Magic Pickle

AND THE GARDEN OF EVIL

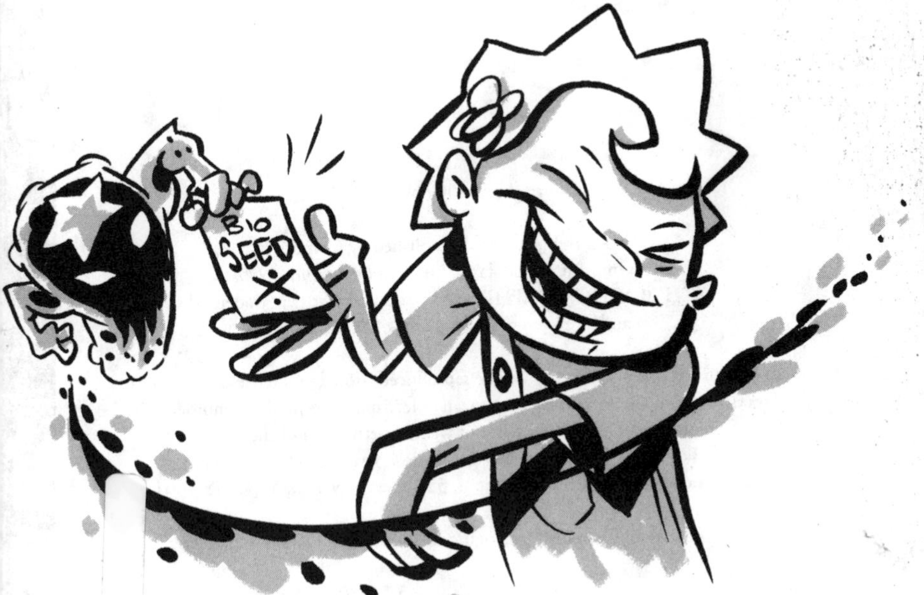
BIO
SEED

BY SCOTT MORSE

A graphix Chapter Book

AN IMPRINT OF
SCHOLASTIC

NEW YORK TORONTO LONDON AUCKLAND SYDNEY MEXICO CITY NEW DELHI HONG KONG BUENOS AIRES

All rights reserved. Published by Graphix,
an imprint of Scholastic Inc., *Publishers since 1920.*
SCHOLASTIC, GRAPHIX, and associated logos are trademarks
and/or registered trademarks of Scholastic Inc.

Library of Congress Cataloging-in-Publication Data is available.

ISBN-13: 978-0-545-13580-1
ISBN-10: 0-545-13580-X

10 9 8 7 6 5 4 3 2 1   09 10 11 12 13

Printed in the U.S.A.   23
First edition, May 2009

Edited by Sheila Keenan
Creative Director: David Saylor
Book design by Charles Kreloff

Prologue

(or everything you need to know before you read this book)

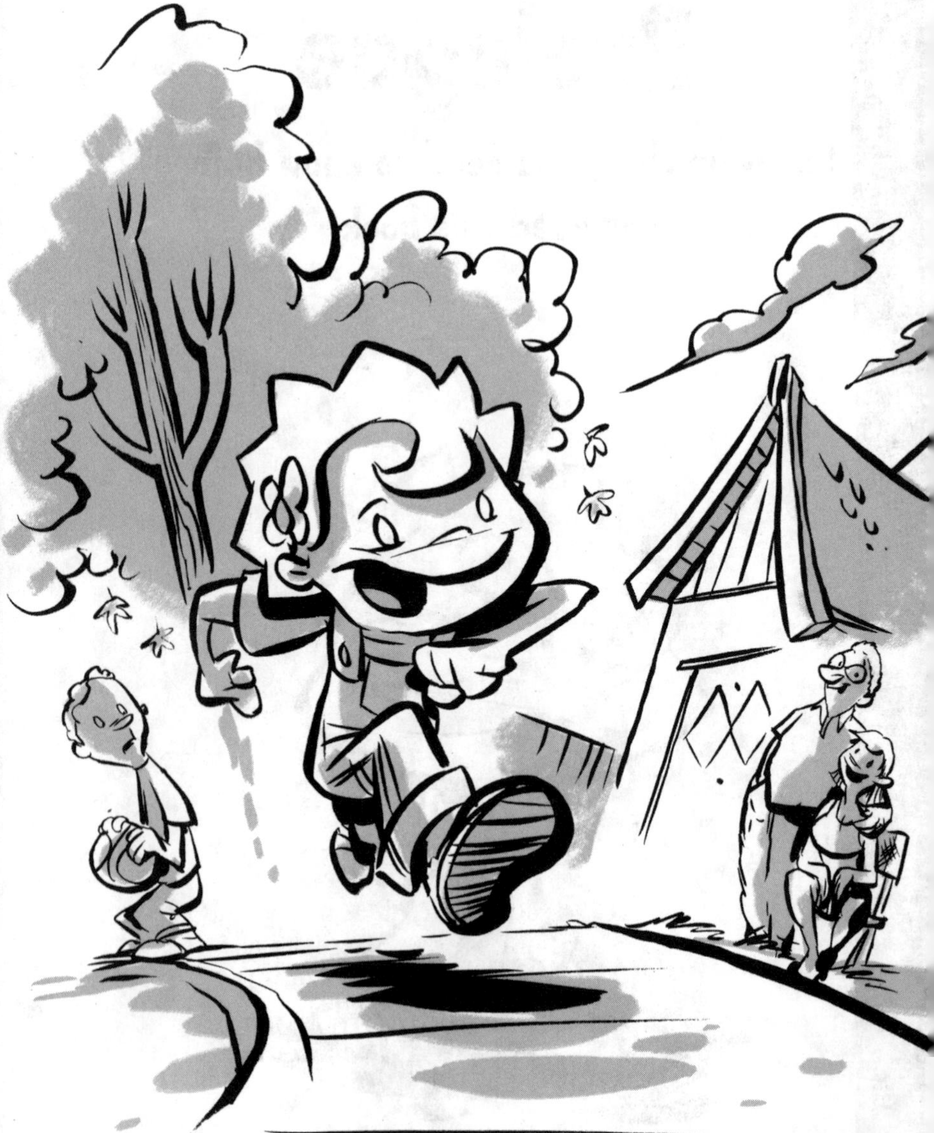

o Jo Wigman was pretty much like any girl you might find sitting near you in class. Her dad was a bigwig at Top Banana Computers and her mom had hair that looked like a big wig (but it was really real). Her brother, Jason, was famous for nothing in particular. He was just goofy. These were all known facts, but Jo Jo had secrets, too, like the one that lived under her seemingly normal house, and more specifically, under her seemingly normal bedroom floor.

A super-powered secret hero.

An agent of dill justice.

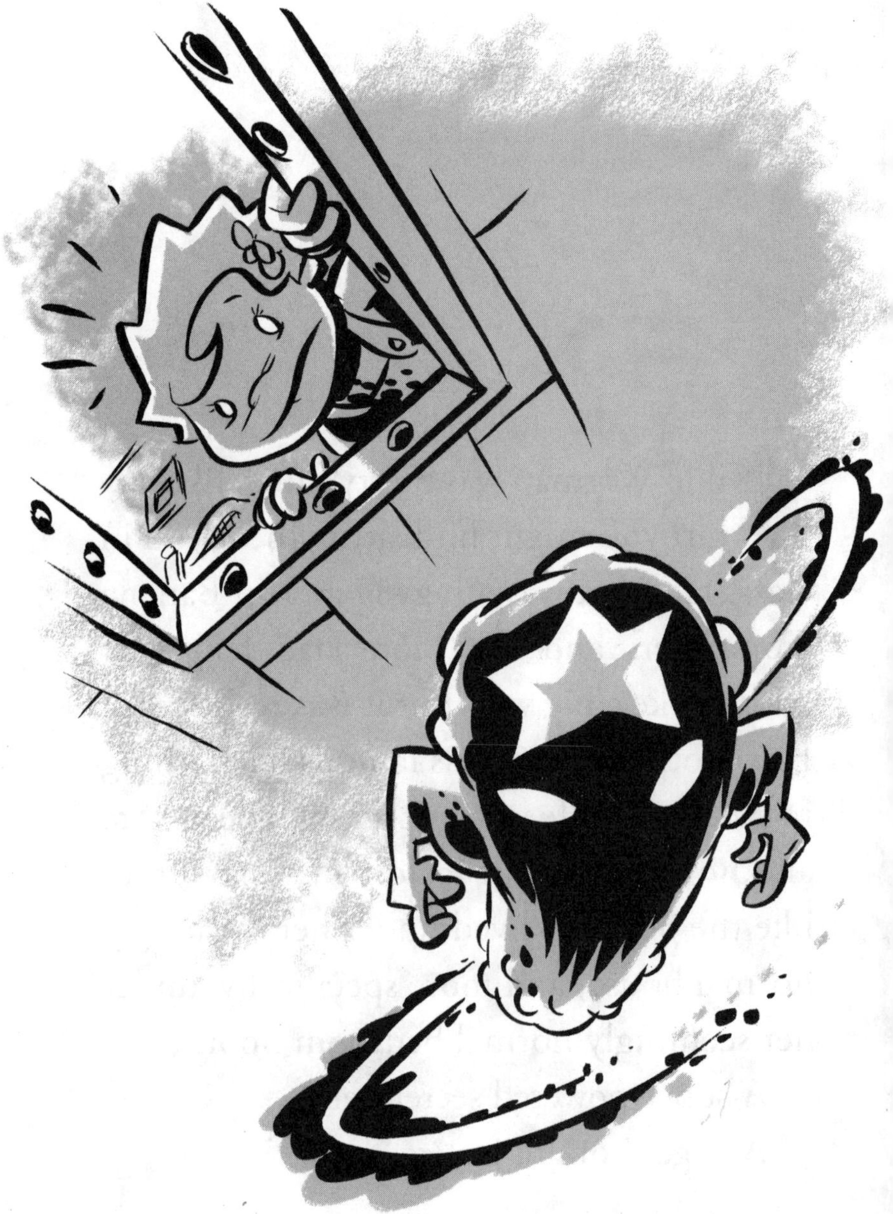

A pickle ... a *talking* pickle!

His government code name was Weapon Kosher, but that just sounded too darn official, so Jo Jo called him Magic Pickle. Magic Pickle's powers weren't actually magical; they were the result of an experiment gone sour. There was this scientist named Dr. Jekyll Formaldehyde who had once worked in a secret government lab called Capital Dill. The Capital Dill lab was so secret that the government built a whole town on top of it. Jo Jo's room was right above the lab!

Dr. Formaldehyde was working on creating a special agent of justice to fight crime and keep the world safe from rotten villains. By accident, the pickle from his lunch fell into the experiment and . . .

KAZZZZORK!!!

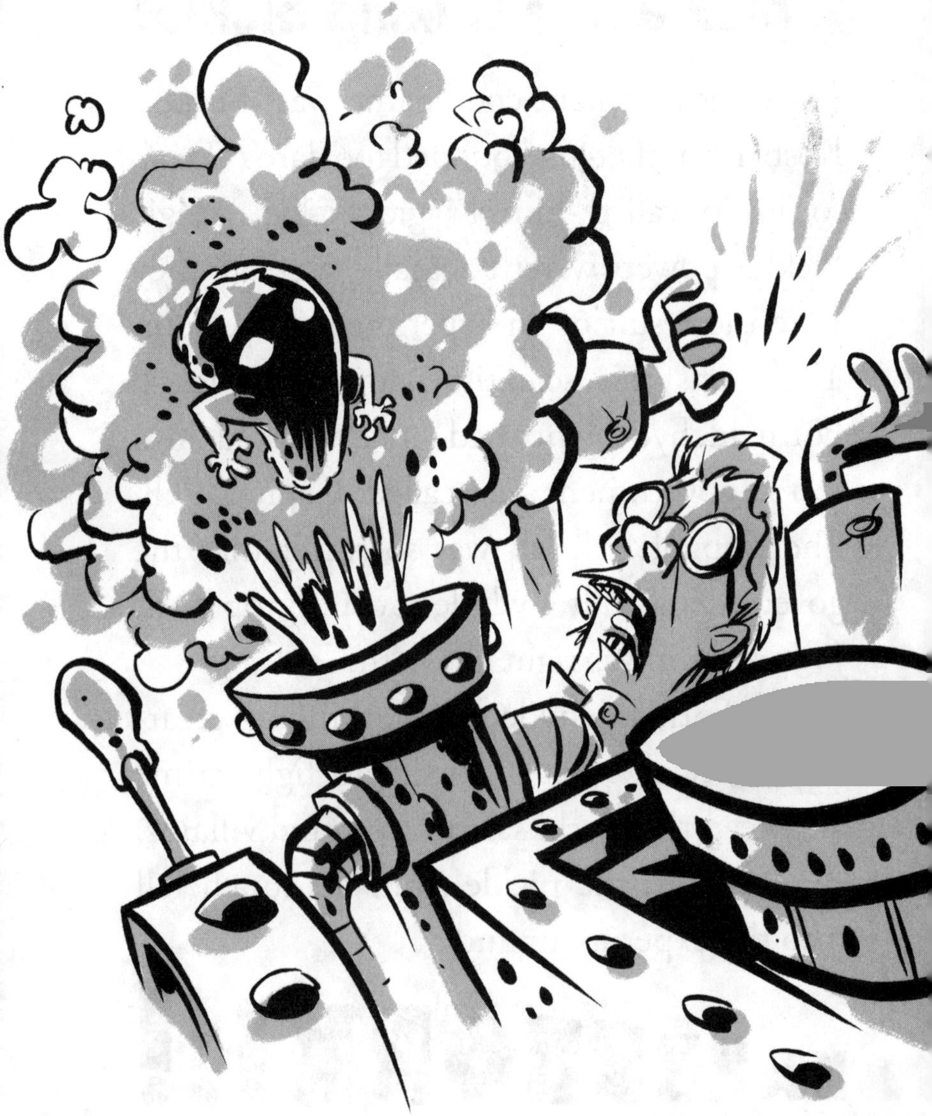

Weapon Kosher was born—but so was something else. . . .

BOOM!

The good doctor's vegetarian combo lunch, which he'd tried to transform into an army of super-powered sidekicks for Weapon Kosher, accidentally went *bad* when the radon rays from the gamma particle confibulator struck the veggies!

Dr. Formaldehyde's dream of creating a legion of super-powered heroes had become a *bad* dream—a nightmare! Dr. F. had accidentally created **THE BROTHERHOOD OF EVIL PRODUCE**! The Brotherhood had only one goal: to take over the world and bring forth the Salad Days, a new age in which fruits and veggies would reign over humankind, forcing people to find some other food group to balance their diets.

The Brotherhood grew larger every minute! Rotten, rancid bad guys joined their ranks: the Phantom Carrot, the Romaine Gladiator, Chili Chili Bang Bang, and more. Only Weapon Kosher could stop these grocery cart convicts!

Dr. Formaldehyde launched himself into space in a special satellite. He circled the earth, tracking the no-good food group and sending news of their tasteless plans back to Weapon Kosher. It was up to Dr. F.'s kosher dill cohort to save the world—from under Jo Jo's bedroom floor!

And that's how Jo Jo came to meet the hush-hush, top-secret, relish-flinging, fast-flying Weapon Kosher who burst up through her bedroom floor. They decided to team up. (Okay, there was some debate about it. Okay, okay, *Jo Jo* decided and she had to talk the

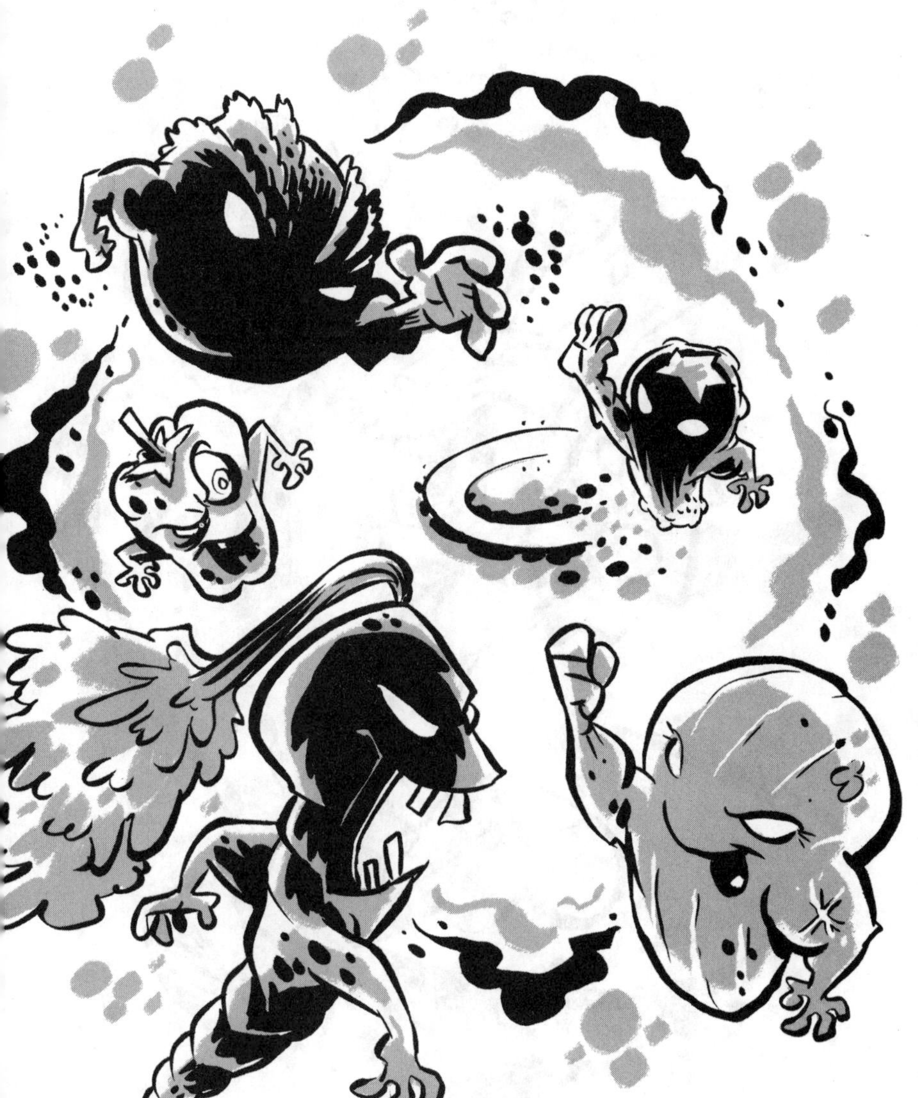

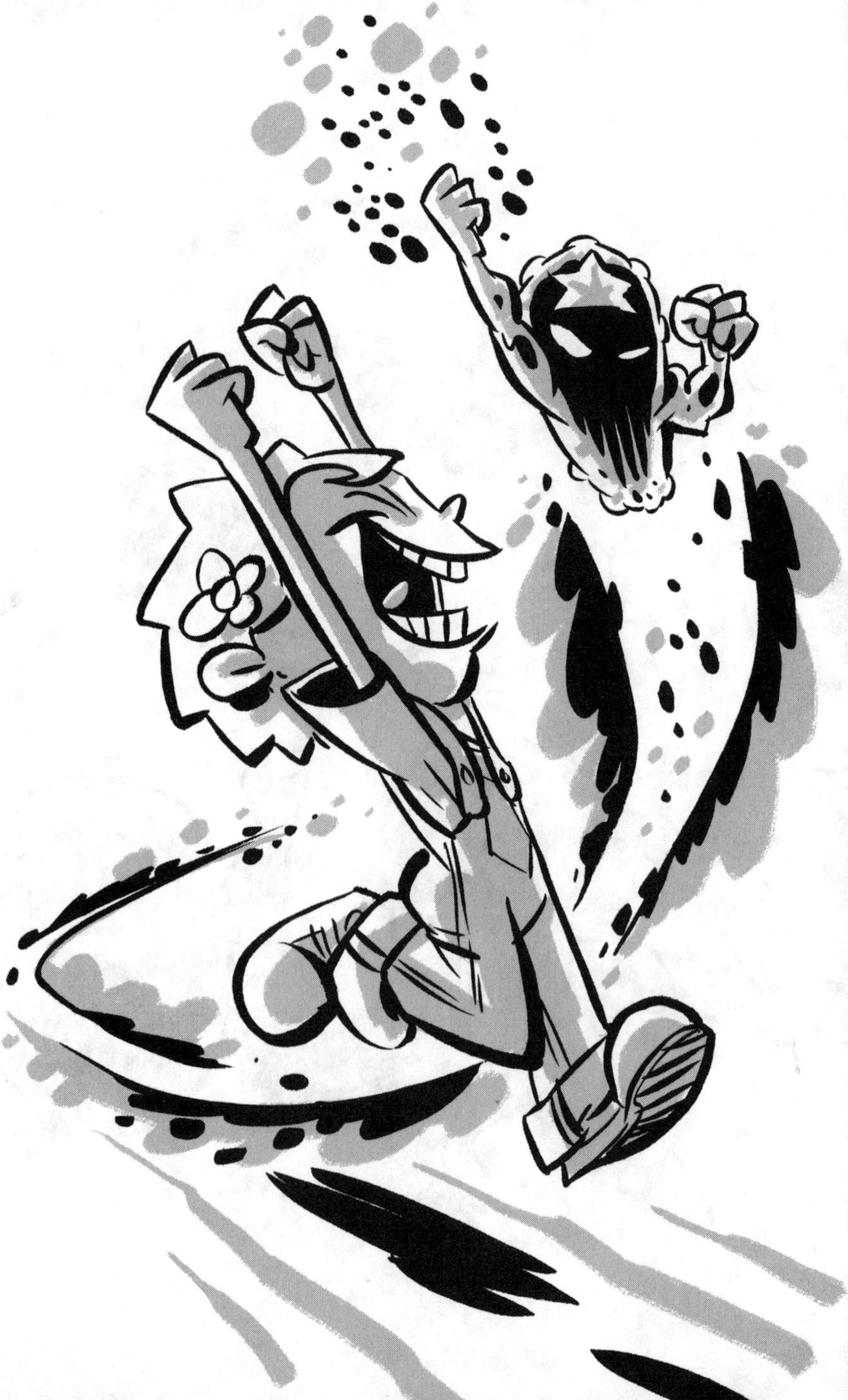

Magic Pickle into it.) Girl and pickle worked together to plow over The Brotherhood of Evil Produce and keep the world safe from evil . . .

. . . but for HOW LONG?

Chapter 1

TAK TAK TAK TAK TAK TAK

Jo Jo tapped a red checker from square to square around the game board, jumping over every last black checker.

"HA! My king has swept the board!" She smiled a snickery smile at her opponent and pulled out a brush and dustpan. "Now it's your turn to sweep. Here. Clean my room!"

"Your tone is threatening and ill-mannered," said the Magic Pickle. "I'll do no such thing."

"We had a deal," Jo Jo insisted, "and you lost the game!"

Jo Jo had planned well: If she lost, she had to wash the jar in which the Magic Pickle slept. If he lost, he had to clean her room! Jo Jo knew how much the Magic Pickle loved a challenge, but he was doomed the minute she took out the checkerboard. He could never resist a game of checkers—and he could never beat Jo Jo!

Magic Pickle sighed. "I've been reduced to being your maid ever since you introduced me to this addictive game of chance."

"It's not a game of chance," said Jo Jo. "It's a game of skill, a game you lost. SWEEP!!!"

"You speak the truth, and as an agent of justice, I must uphold the truth. But I find it downright deceptive and cruel that you'd take advantage of my inferior game skills," the Magic Pickle told her. "Either way, you planned all along to trick me into doing your chores."

"Come on!" Jo Jo laughed. "I even let you be *black*, the cool color!"

The Magic Pickle paused.

"That is beside the point," he said. "Red is the color of anger and rage. No law-enforcing agent of justice would ever agree to play red."

"Whatever. A deal's a deal, you lost, now CLEAN!"

In a green, pulsing glow, the Magic Pickle flew around Jo Jo's room, tossing dirty clothes into her hamper and tucking in the edges of her bedspread. He swept the room in a briny flash.

"Lookin' good, ya lean, mean greenie," Jo Jo called. "Lookin' good. Mom said if my room was spick-and-span before I left for school this morning she'd think about letting me get a pet!"

"Out of the question!" said the Magic Pickle. "An animal would compromise our defenses! Villains would no doubt attempt to bribe their way into my secret lair with promises of tasty treats! A dog would fall victim to the cries of its stomach if offered a steak, and a cat would bend for much less, a ball of yarn, or—"

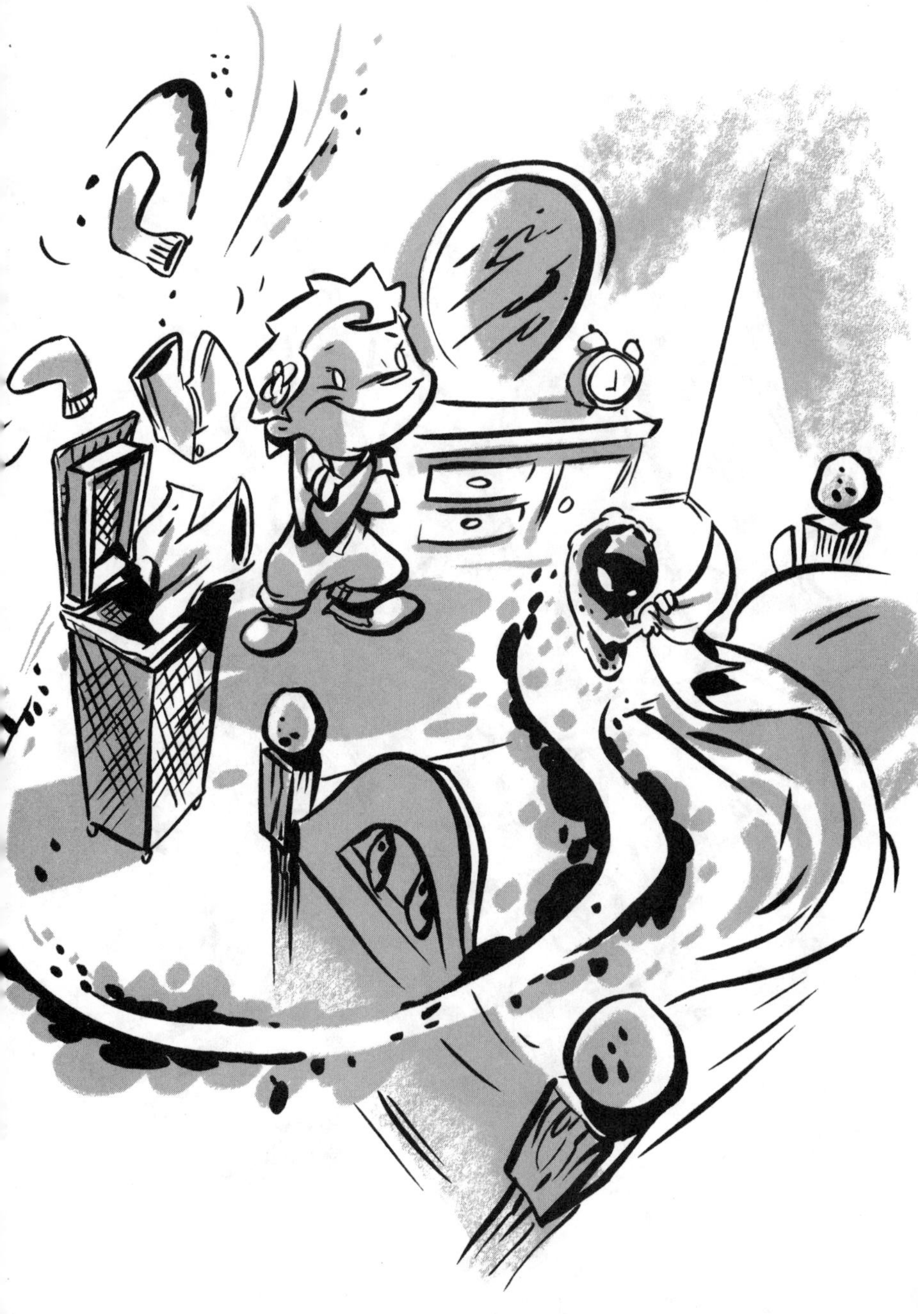

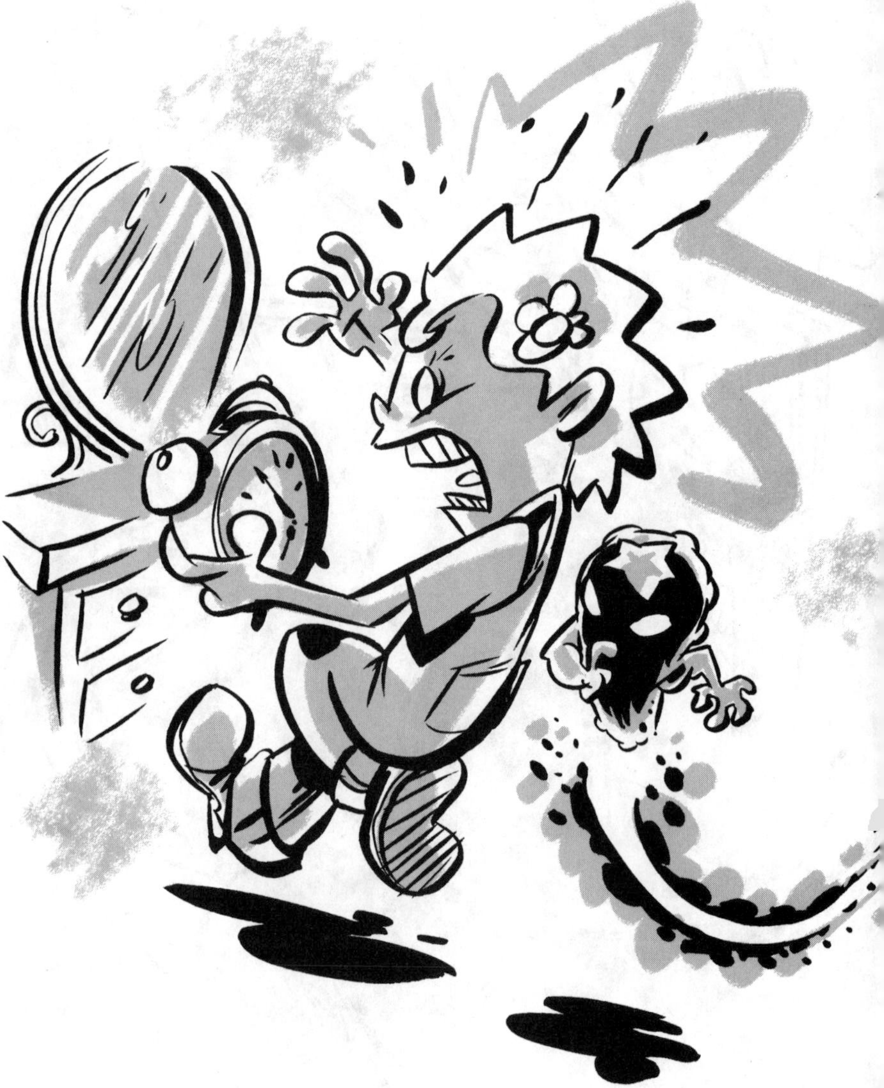

"Calm down, calm down," Jo Jo assured him. "I was thinking of a goldfish!"

"Inconceivable!" the Magic Pickle replied. "Goldfish are a menace, always swimming in circles, planning their escape from their bowls!"

Jo Jo looked at the clock and gasped.

"I'm going to be late for school!" she gulped. "Don't forget to dust my lampshade!"

"Maybe you should bring home a pet rabbit," suggested the Magic Pickle. "He could use his ears to dust the high spots."

"Maybe I will!" Jo Jo smiled and ducked out the door.

"I WAS JOKING!" shouted the Magic Pickle.

Chapter 2

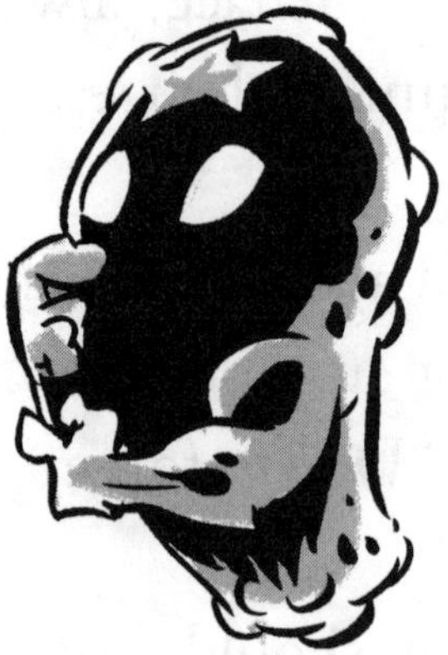

"You people are going to love me forever!" Mikey Spuchins stood at the front of the classroom. He tried to high-five his fellow students as they wandered to their desks.

BBBBRRRRIINNNNNNGGGG!!!

The morning bell rang just as Jo Jo and her best friend, Ellen Cranston, slid into their seats. Jo Jo shot a look at Ellen: Why on Earth was Mikey Spuchins standing up there with their teacher, Miss Emilyek? And why was his smile so darn big?

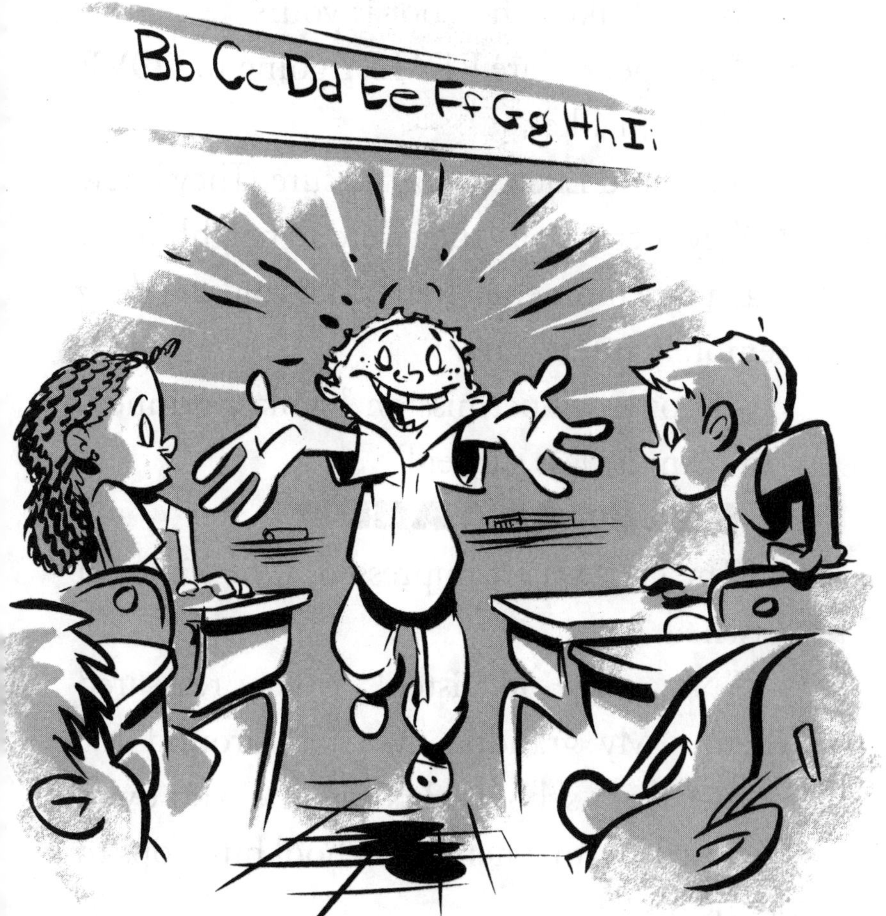
Bb Cc Dd Ee Ff Gg Hh Ii

Ellen returned the look and shrugged. She was just as confused as Jo Jo.

"Class, Mikey has a special announcement for everyone," Miss Emilyek announced. "Go on, Mikey, the floor is yours."

"You people are REALLY going to LOVE me!" said Mikey.

Jo Jo and Ellen weren't so sure. They knew Mikey pretty well. They were all neighbors. It was a rare moment when Mikey did *anything* remotely interesting.

"I got us all permission," Mikey grinned, "to plant a class garden!"

GRRROOAAANNN

The class wasn't impressed. One kid even yawned.

"No, come on, listen!" Mikey reassured them. "My grandpa lives just around the corner from school! He's the one who owns that little farm where the school bus stops to let us out!"

Jo Jo raised an eyebrow. There was indeed a little farm around the corner from school. Every kid in town knew the place, mainly because they were never allowed in there. It was really just a big backyard, fenced in. In the fall, you could see the tips of cornstalks peeking just over the top of the fence that separated the farm from the school.

"Now, class," said Miss Emilyek. "Mikey's grandfather has agreed to let us use our science hour each day to plant a class garden and keep track of the growth of our crops. This is a very special treat. You'll all be allowed to participate and help our garden grow strong."

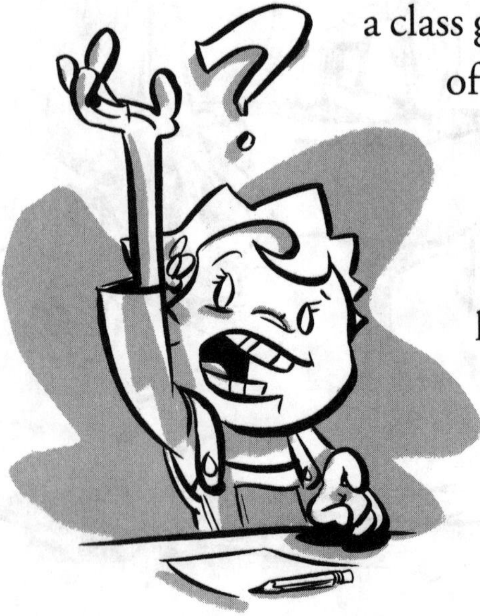

Jo Jo raised her hand.

"What are we going to plant?" she asked.

"I had an idea about that," said Miss Emilyek. "It's actually your homework assignment. I'd like you each to research and find the right plants for our area. Then bring in your choice of seeds this week. We'll plant them all and see what grows best."

"Anything we want?" asked Ellen.

"Anything as long as it's a vegetable or an herb," answered Miss Emilyek. "That's part of your homework, to research and find the perfect seed."

"Don't you LOVE it?!" Mikey screamed.

All the students in his class rolled their eyes at once. How could you love anything that involves *homework*?!

Chapter 3

"**C**ome on, just one seed!" Jo Jo begged.

"Out of the question," the Magic Pickle answered flatly.

Jo Jo had been rummaging through the archives of a small room in Capital Dill behind a door with a big sign stenciled on it:

G.R.O.W.

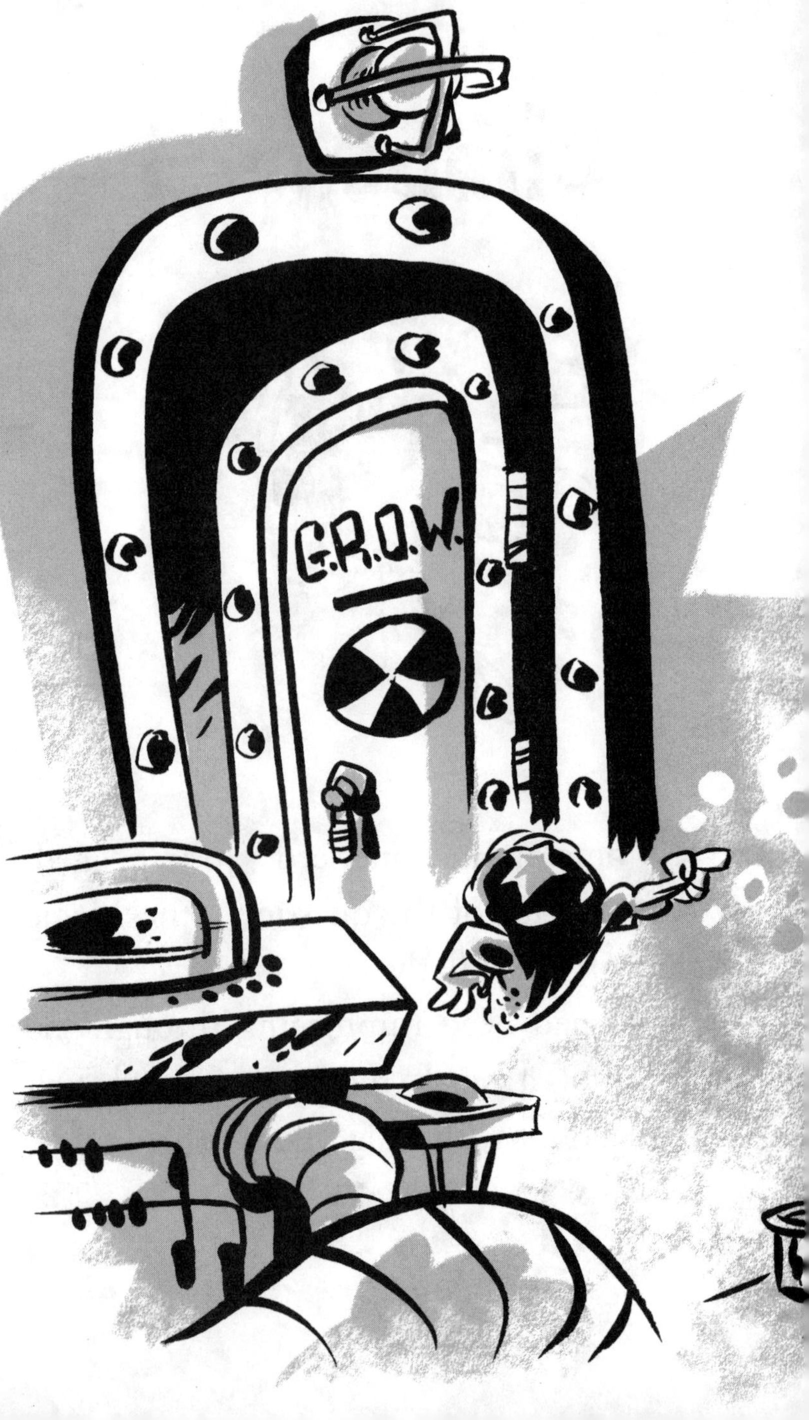
G.R.O.W.

The Magic Pickle usually kept the room locked.

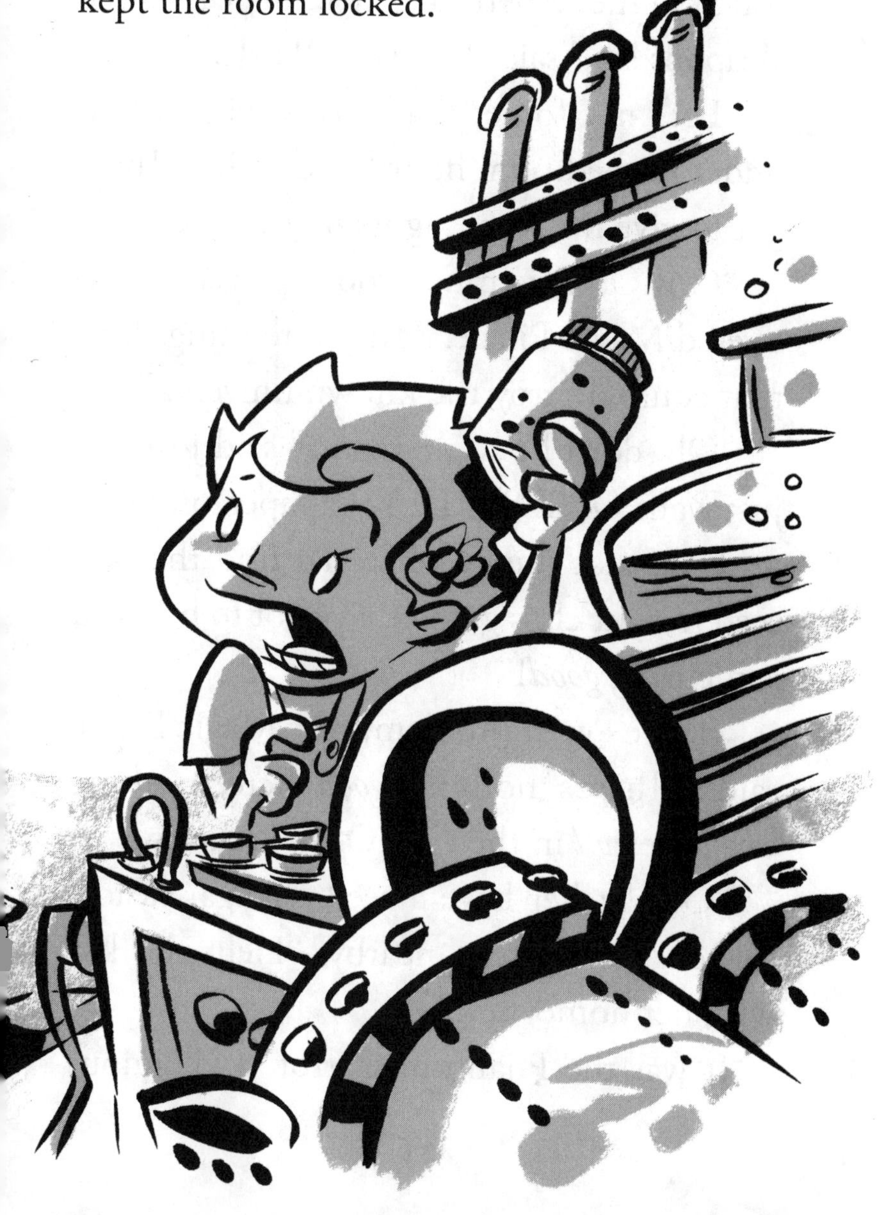

"I knew I shouldn't have let you do any research in the **G**enetic **R**egeneratory **O**rganized **W**eapons lab," said the Magic Pickle.

"Let's not forget that this whole place is under *my* bedroom floor," said Jo Jo. "That's got to give me some rights here, right?"

"G.R.O.W. is much too top-secret," answered Magic Pickle. "There are things here that could destroy the known universe."

"Oh, don't be so dramatic," said Jo Jo. "I just want ONE SEED! Your supercomputer told me that this is where I'd find the best seed for our class garden! I've got to bring in something *good*!"

"There's your problem," the Magic Pickle said. "There's nothing *good* here, nothing but pure *evil* in the G.R.O.W. archives."

"Oh, let her have a seed, vinegar head!" called a voice from nearby. "Help the kid with her homework!"

It was the Phantom Carrot, a villainous

scoundrel who had recently been locked up by the Magic Pickle. Jo Jo had helped MP round up most of The Brotherhood of Evil Produce during a big battle at her school. The Phantom Carrot, Chili Chili Bang Bang, Squish Squash, Pea Shooter, they'd all been locked up in the Deep Freeze. Only one villain wasn't in this prison block in Capital Dill: the Romaine Gladiator. He'd come to a nasty end in the school cafeteria's garbage disposal, flushed away into the compost heap behind the building.

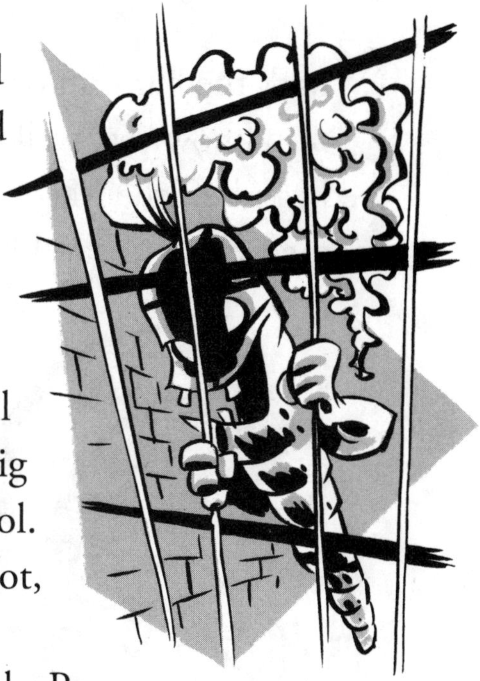

"Go on, let her have one!" The Phantom Carrot snickered from behind his bars.

"What's the harm in one little seed?"

"You know very well how destructive one seed can be," the Magic Pickle growled. He zoomed close to the Phantom Carrot's cell and glowered at the frilly-headed root. "One seed is all it takes to grow a villain like you."

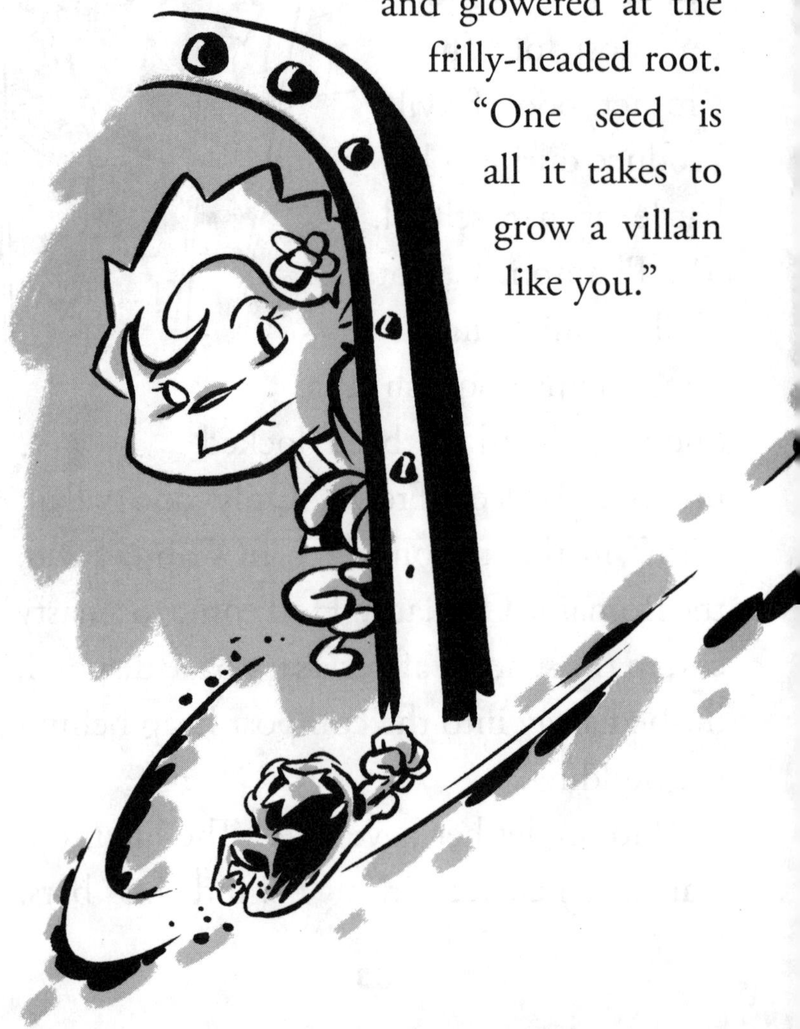

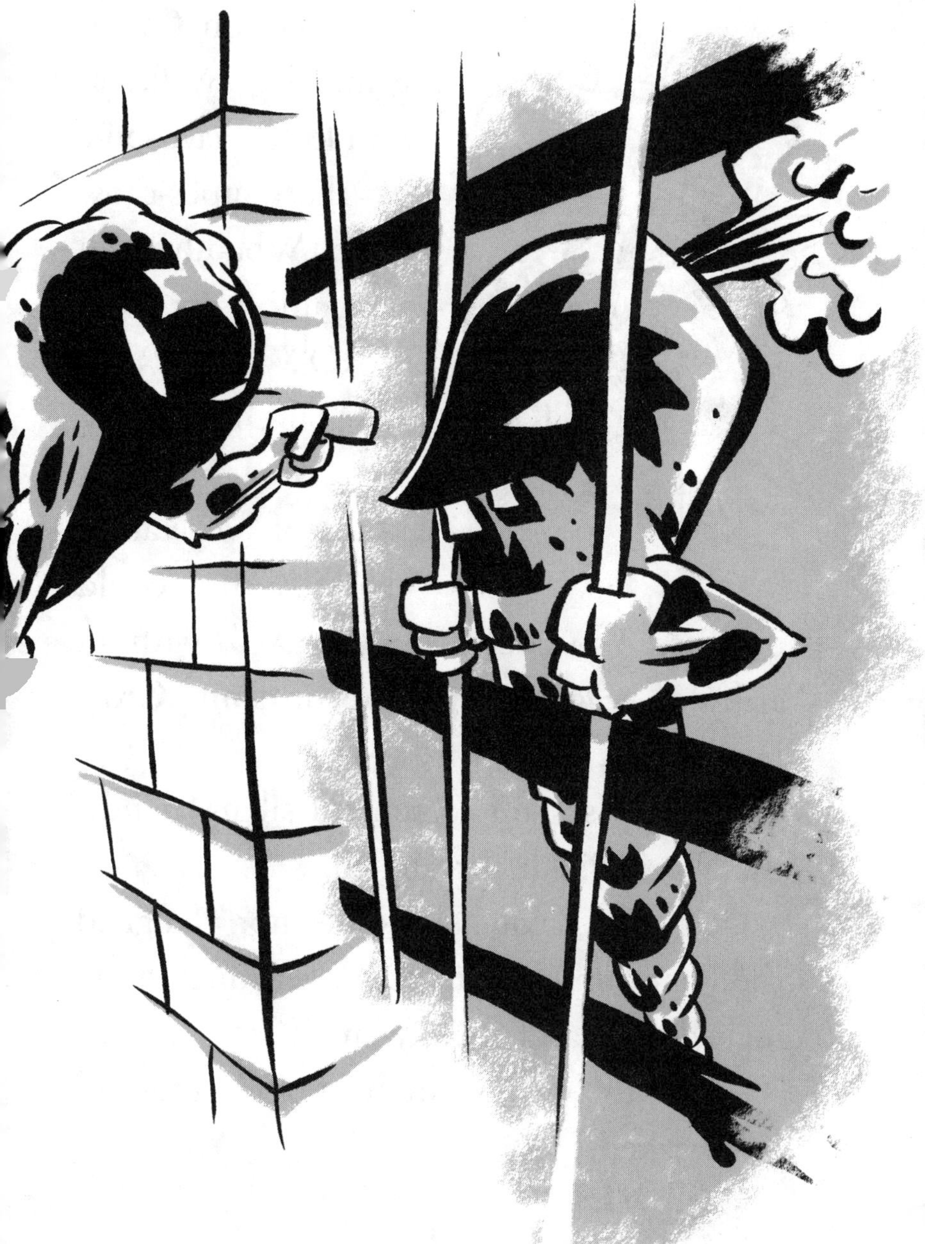

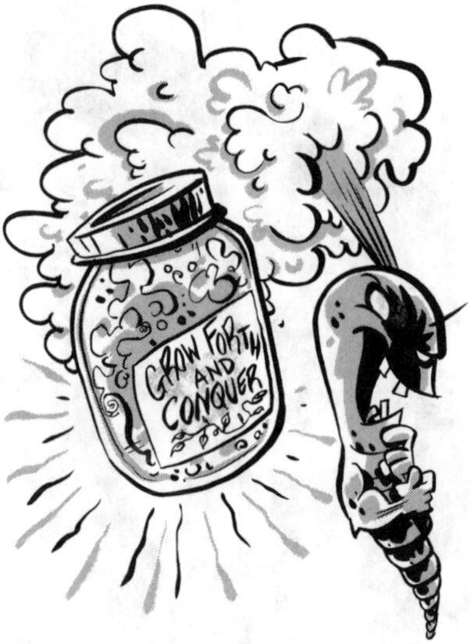
GROW FORTH AND CONQUER

The Phantom Carrot grinned. "Well, at least let her have some of that super-grow juice. Whaddya call it again? Oh, yeah: 'GROW FORTH AND CONQUER.' Man, imagine what kind of vegetation that stuff could produce! You could rule the *world* with an army of veggies amped up on some Grow Forth and Conquer. . . ."

"I'd advise you to remain silent, fiend," the Magic Pickle threatened.

"Or what, you'll lock me up?" laughed the Phantom Carrot. "Can't get much more locked up than I already am!"

"What's 'Grow Forth and Conquer'?" Jo Jo asked.

"A very strong secret compound used to amplify the growth process of vegetable matter," the Magic Pickle informed her. "You will be getting *none*."

"Aww, man," whined Jo Jo. Then she had an idea. "I'll play you a game of *checkers* for some . . . ?"

"Yeah! Why don't you play her a game a *checkers* for it?" urged the Phantom Carrot.

The Magic Pickle frowned in frustration as Jo Jo set up the game board. He fought the urge to rise to Jo Jo's challenge, but the thrill of moving those black and red chips around the board haunted him for some reason. He tried to resist, turning his head away.

But those chips . . . those wonderfully symbolic checkers chips.

They called to him with their shiny red and black colors.

The board itself was like a puzzle waiting to be unlocked, a puzzle that only the most clever could piece together into a WIN.

His eyes tried to look away, but the lure of the game pulled them back.

His fingers tried to stay by his side, clenched in fists, but to no avail. His green digits unfolded and crept toward the black chips.

"You drive a hard bargain, girl," the Magic Pickle said—as he moved his first black checker across the board.

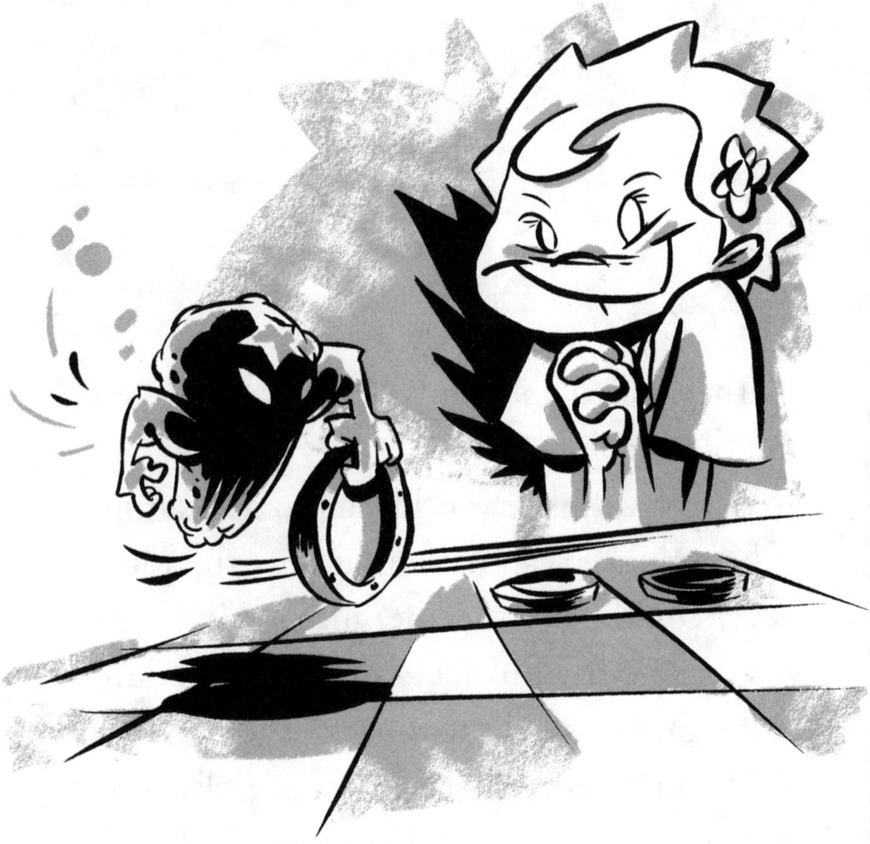

Chapter 4

"**C**lass, let's all thank Mr. Spuchins for the use of his farm," said Miss Emilyek.

"Thanks, Farmer Spuchins," the students sang out.

The entire class stood in a cluster near a big plot of freshly tilled soil. They each held a paper name tag pasted to the end of a craft

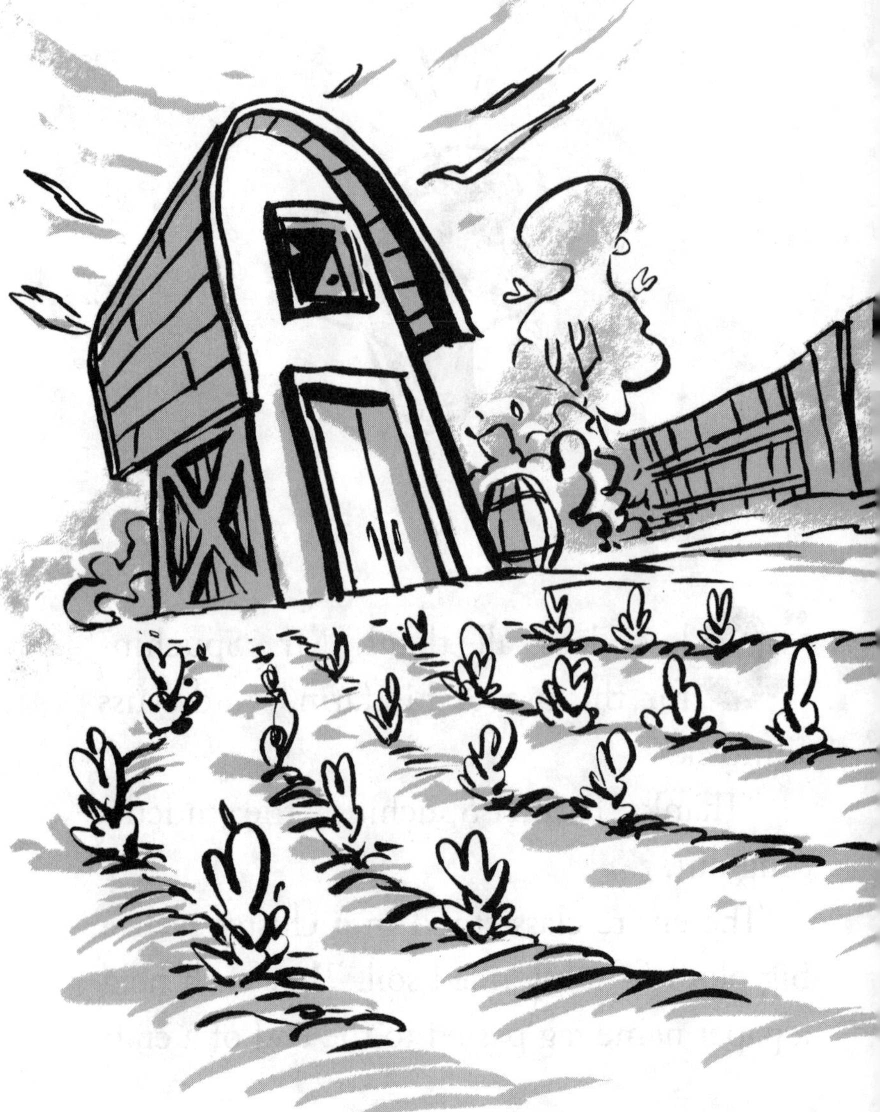

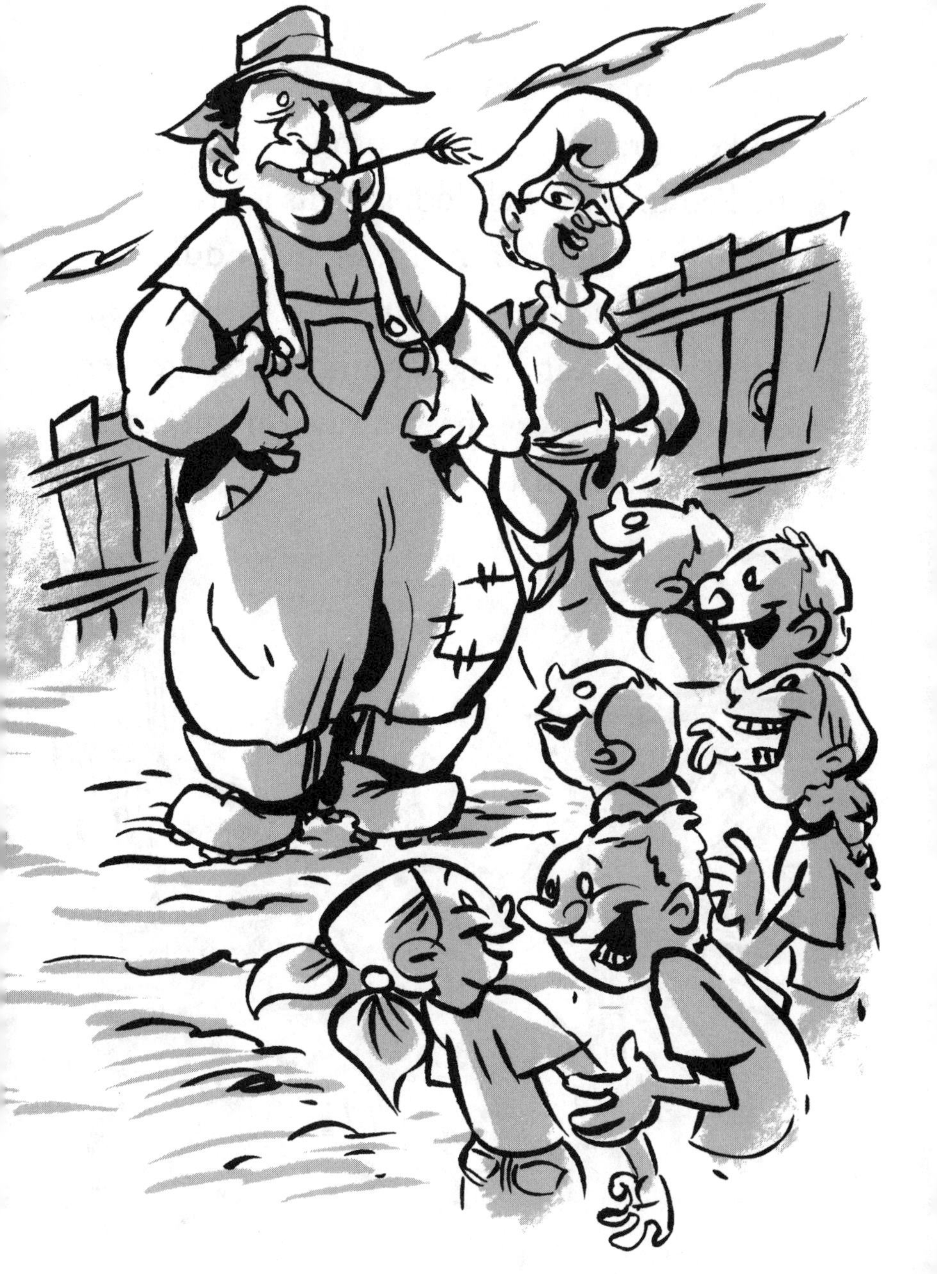

stick to mark their own section of the garden. Mikey's grandpa stood by proudly, his thumbs tucked into the belt loops of his jeans.

Jo Jo, Ellen, and Mikey sat huddled on an old tree stump near the class garden. They were watching rabbits in a huge pen along the fence gnaw away on pieces of celery and carrot.

"How CUTE!" said Ellen.

Jo Jo tried to pet a rabbit through the cage front with one finger. "Here, boy."

"My grandpa keeps 'em as pets," said Mikey. "They're kind of stinky. So what are you going to grow?"

"Check *these* out," Ellen said. She held out a fistful of tiny seeds. They were long and thin like rice, only pointier.

"What are they?" asked Jo Jo.

"I have no idea!" Ellen replied. "I grabbed

them from my mom's gardening shed before I got on the bus."

"Didn't spend much time on the homework, eh?" asked Jo Jo.

"I did!" said Mikey. He shrugged. "But I forgot my seeds at home. Good thing there's that compost heap out behind the cafeteria. I scrounged some seeds out of the dirt. Look."

Jo Jo and Ellen gagged and covered their mouths and noses.

BLLEEECCCHHH!!!

Mikey's seeds were shriveled and hard and yellowed like old newspapers. They smelled horrible, like old wet socks that had been walking on yucky movie theater floors. Movie theaters playing *horror films.*

"Mikey, those seeds don't look like they'll grow *anything,*" said Ellen.

"At least not anything I'd eat," said Jo Jo.

"Oh, come on, Ellen!" Mikey pleaded. "Just let me plant my seeds next to yours. Maybe your plants will spill over. We'll say we grew the same thing! No one'll know. . . ."

Jo Jo pulled a small container of liquid from the pocket of her overalls.

"Maybe this'll help," she suggested.

"What is it?" Ellen wondered with a raised eyebrow.

The liquid swirled and wisped around the

inside of the glass container like smoke or creepy fog. Then it dripped down the sides of the glass like gurgley gluey goo, first yellow and purple like a bruise, then orange and pink like a delicious peach or something. Ellen and Mikey couldn't take their eyes off of the stuff.

"It's plant food I brought from home," said Jo Jo. It was actually the easily won prize of her most recent checkers match with the Magic Pickle, but how would she ever explain *that* to Ellen and Mikey?

"You mean you didn't bring any seeds?!" asked Ellen. "That was the homework assignment!"

"I know, but I figured this plant food might be better," said Jo Jo. "I made it myself from an old family recipe. It's got to be worth a bunch of extra credit. It'll help our plants grow *faster*!"

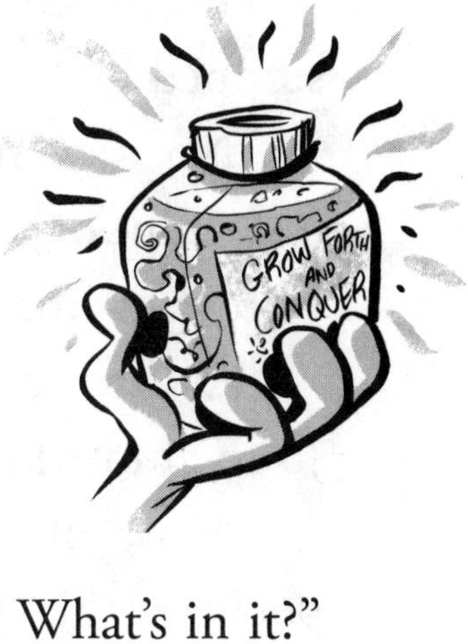
GROW FORTH
AND
CONQUER

"What do you call it?" Mikey asked. "Does it have a cool name? Can *I* name it?"

"It's, uh, it's got a name already," Jo Jo remembered. "Grow Forth and Conquer."

"That's SO COOL! Like a *garden warrior* or something! What's in it?" Mikey wondered aloud.

"Oh, you know," Jo Jo muttered, looking

around nervously, trying to change the subject, "just some, uh . . . there's . . .well, there's pickle juice, and some celery salt, and some, uh, mustard, I think. . . ."

"I've got a bad feeling about this," said Ellen.

Jo Jo dug a small hole with her trowel. Ellen dumped her seeds into the hole; Mikey moved forward to do the same. Ellen stopped him.

"No way. Your seeds look diseased. Our only hope of getting a good grade is the seeds *I* brought from home."

"AND the Grow Forth and Conquer!" Jo Jo chimed in.

"Aww, all right," Mikey whined. He pocketed his pile of rotten seeds. "But at least cover for me and say I planted some seeds with you, okay?"

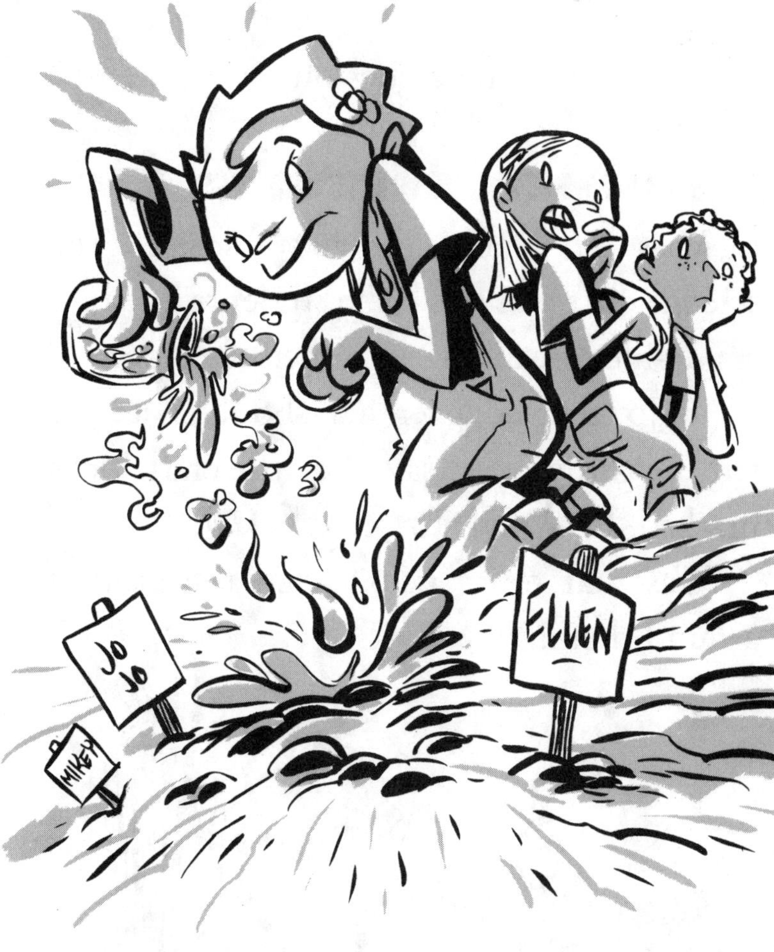
JO JO
MIKEY
ELLEN

"Whatever." Ellen covered her seeds with dirt and patted them gently. Jo Jo uncorked her glass container and dripped the mysterious liquid onto the ground.

"Here goes nothing," she said.

"You mean 'there goes our assignment!'" said Ellen.

TWWWEEEEEEEETT

Miss Emilyek blew her whistle. The science class was over. The students lined up single-file to walk back to their classroom.

Jo Jo glanced over her shoulder as she left the garden. She saw the little craft sticks marked **JO JO**, **MIKEY**, and **ELLEN**.

Was that *steam* rising from the ground around them?

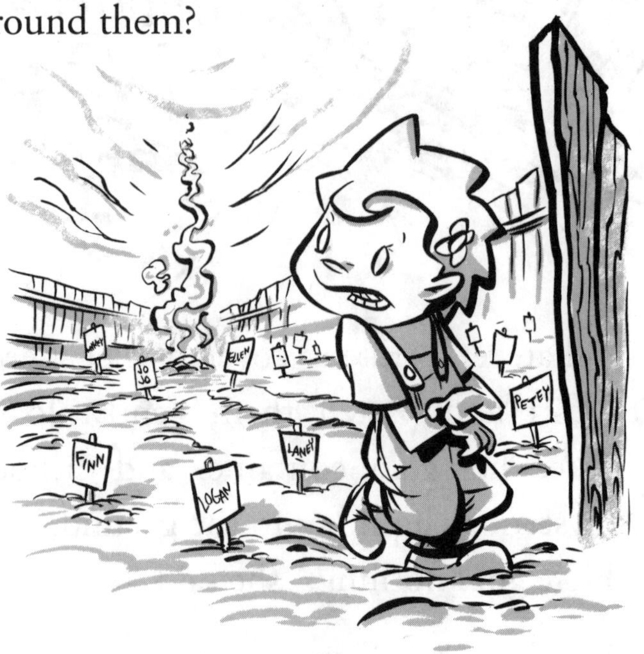

LANEY
JO JO
ELLEN
PETEY
FINN
LANEY
LOGAN

Chapter 5

"What a loser . . ." said the Phantom Carrot.

The Magic Pickle muttered and continued to research checkers moves on his supercomputer.

"There must be *some* trick she's using," the Magic Pickle said to himself. He played back the video of his last match with Jo Jo. He

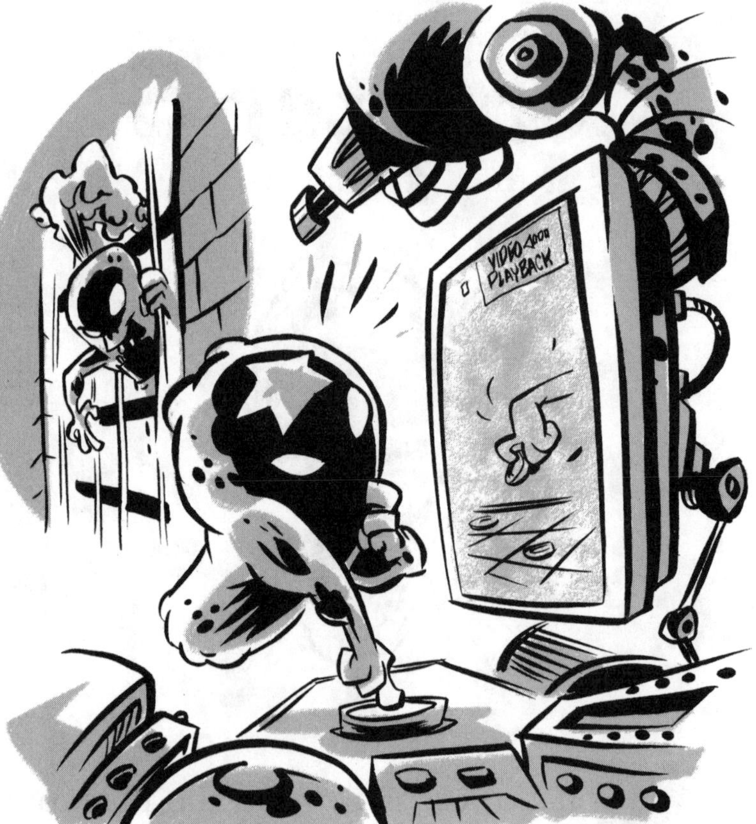
VIDEO 4000
PLAYBACK

tried to record everything that went down in the dark halls of Capital Dill, just in case. The video showed nothing suspicious. Jo Jo played fairly.

"I'LL show you how to play checkers," said the Phantom Carrot.

"You'll do no such thing," the Magic Pickle snapped. "First, you're evil compressed into carrot form and not worth a checkers match. Second, I've got a superior mind and would mulch you with my first move on the checkerboard."

"Well, OH HO HO!" replied the Phantom Carrot. "Surely those two points are reason enough for us to play!"

"How do you figure that?" questioned the Magic Pickle.

"Well, first, with my being *evil* and all, it's your sworn duty to face me at every challenge!" said the Phantom Carrot. "And second, what have you got to lose, if you're really smarter than me? I'm already your prisoner."

Hmmm, thought the Magic Pickle. He glanced at the checkerboard. He was hypnotized by the squares. They were calling his name . . . calling him to a game.

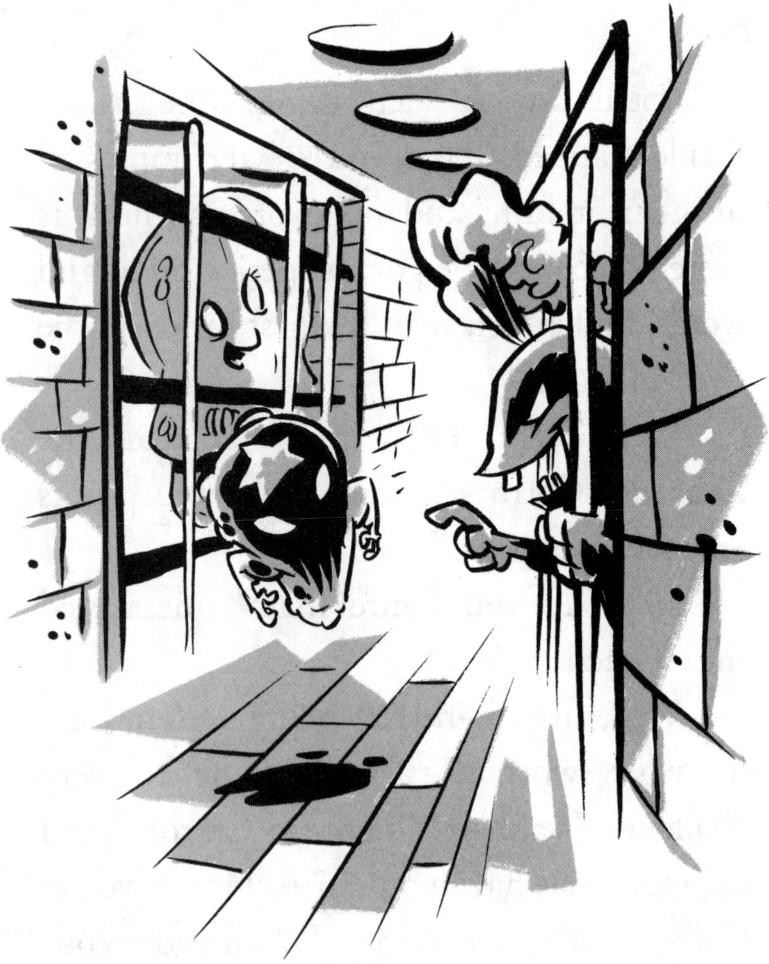

"Play him!" squealed Squish Squash, the big oafish vegetable in the next cell.

"Yeah, play him," called Chili Chili Bang Bang from a neighboring cell. "And make it *interesting:* If that big carrot top loses, we'll all stop teasing you every time you float by. But if he *wins* . . ."

"Impossible," scoffed the Magic Pickle.

"So says *you*. But *if* Phantom *wins,* you let us *all* out for some fresh air," continued Chili Chili Bang Bang. "Just for a few minutes."

The Phantom Carrot grinned his crooked teeth at the Magic Pickle.

"He ain't brave enough fer a challenge like *that*," the Phantom Carrot boasted. "I mean, seriously. He looks kinda *sick,* even. Look how *green* he is!"

"ENOUGH!" shouted the Magic Pickle. He slapped a switch and the Phantom Carrot's cell door slid open. The Magic Pickle floated the checkerboard over in front of the open cell. "I'm black. Red is for villainous scoundrels like you—"

"HA HA HA!"

the Phantom Carrot laughed. "I don't even have to move a checker and *YOU LOSE*!"

FWOOSH!

The Phantom Carrot disappeared.

"What the—?" the Magic Pickle gasped in shock. "He disappeared!"

"Well, he *is* the *Phantom* Carrot," reminded Pea Shooter from a cell down the hall. "What'd you expect? A fair game?"

"DRAT!" The Magic Pickle scowled. "I forgot his spectral distortion energy was dampened by his cell, but once that cell door opened . . . If only I had more self-control! I can never turn my back on those red and black chips! Checkers is a vile temptress! CURSE this game!"

Magic Pickle zapped the checkerboard with a blast of green particles.

FGZOORRKK!

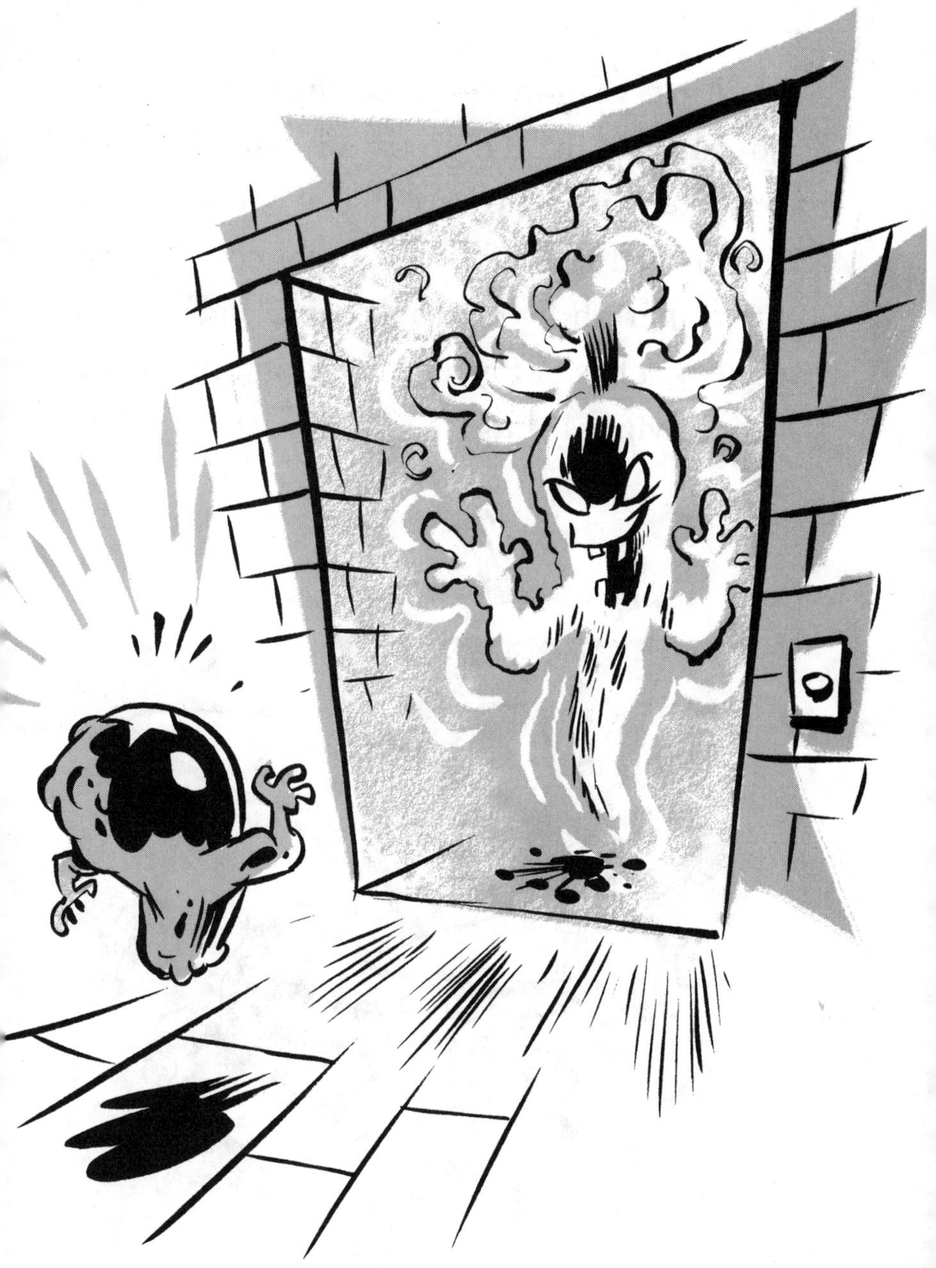

"Ain't ya gonna go catch him?" asked Squish Squash. "I'd go try an' catch him if I was like you and wasn't all evil and—"

But before Squish Squash could even finish her thought, the Magic Pickle was gone in a flash of green. Nothing but a faint hint of vinegar lingered in the air.

Chapter 6

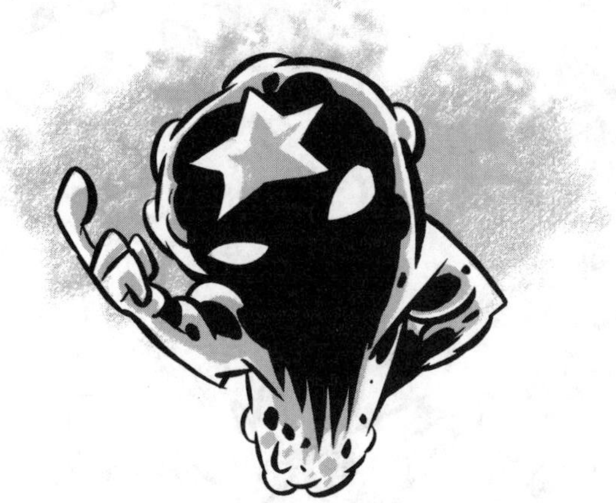

BBBBRRRIINNNNNNGGGG!!!

School was over for the day. Jo Jo and Ellen grabbed their backpacks and headed for the door. Mikey caught up with them.

"Hey, guys, let's go check on the garden, huh?" Mikey suggested. "I bet we've already got, like, sprouts and stuff coming out of the dirt!"

"Mikey, come on," said Ellen. "We just planted the seeds yesterday. You know plants don't grow that fast."

"But it's my grandpa's farm!" Mikey gaped. "His dirt's like MAGIC! He's always growing way more stuff than he can sell at the market. Plus, we drenched those seeds in Jo Jo's Grow Forth and Conquer juice! It'll be like a plant ARMY in there!"

"Umm, let's hope not," Jo Jo murmured, worried. There was no telling what sort of effect that stuff might be having. And then there was that steam . . .

"We can walk by on our way home and peek in," she said.

"Fine," said Ellen. "But nature is nature, and plants only grow so fast."

Jo Jo, Ellen, and Mikey walked across the school grounds and rounded the corner to Grandpa Spuchins' farm. It looked a lot shadier, like clouds were passing in front of the sun. Jo Jo looked up. Her eyes widened.

Huge, frilly-fringed leaves grew high over the farm's fence, casting long shadows like trees.

"Whu-oh," said Jo Jo under her breath.

"Oh, MAN!" Mikey shouted. "Look at THAT!"

"Did your grandpa plant some palm trees after we went back to class?!" asked Ellen.

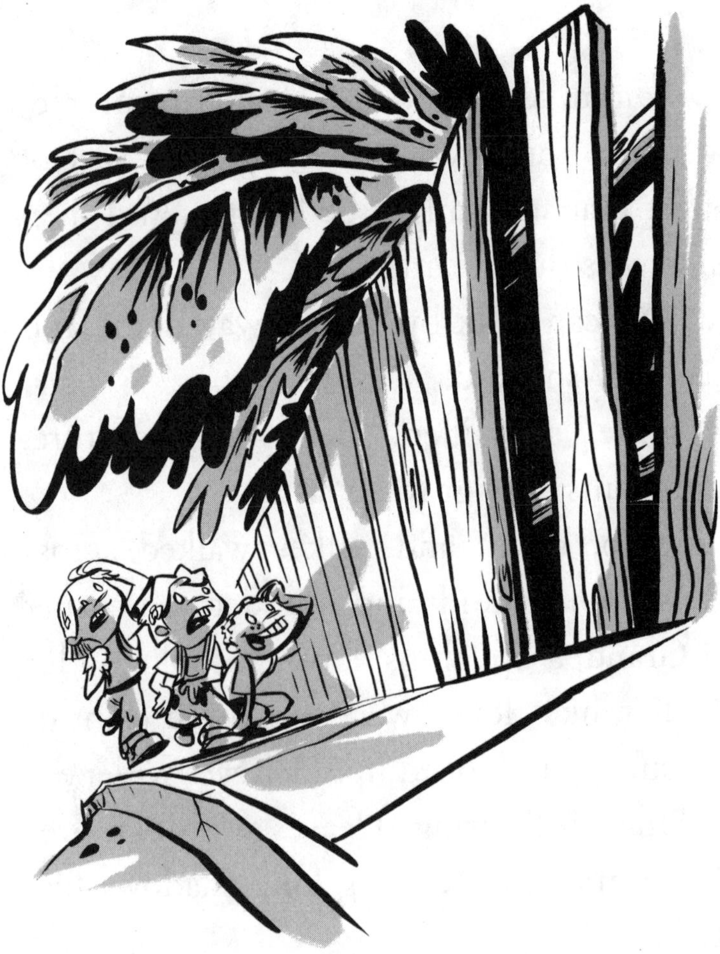

The three hurried into the garden and headed straight for their plot. A huge, towering plant grew right out of the spot where Jo Jo had sprinkled the Grow Forth and Conquer.

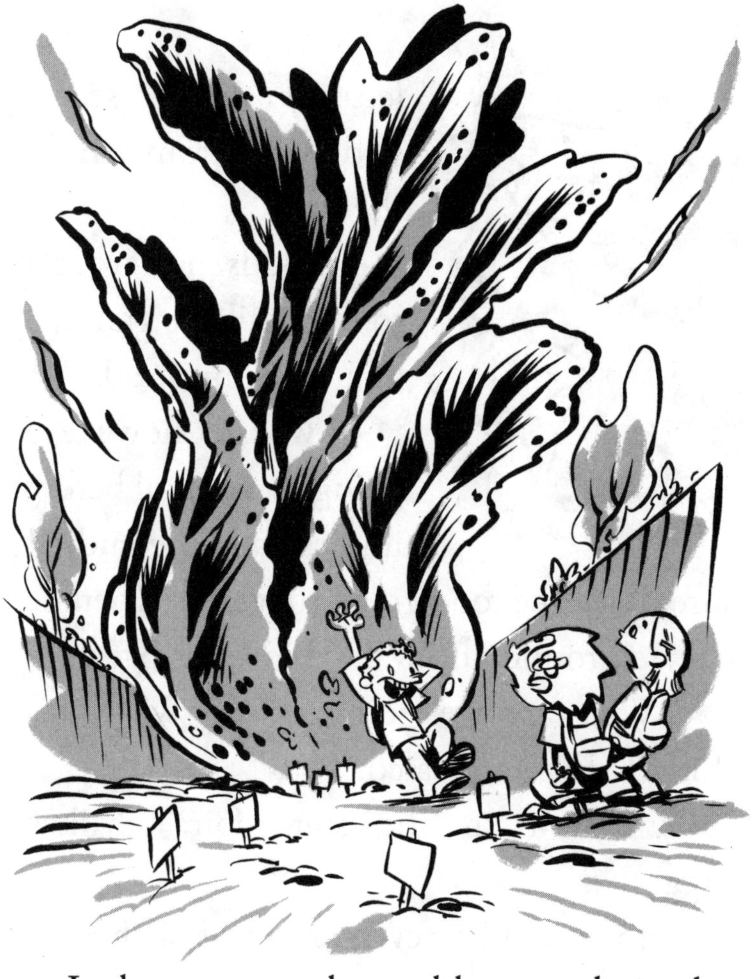

Its humongous leaves blew gently in the wind. They could feel the draft from five feet away.

"What is THAT?!" cried Ellen.

"*That* is the BIGGEST HEAD of romaine

lettuce *I've* ever seen," said a voice from behind them.

The kids spun around to find Mikey's grandpa scratching his head.

"I wonder how we're going to eat it all before it goes bad?" he said. "I sure don't like food going to waste." Then he turned around and walked into his barn.

"What are we going to do with this thing?!" Ellen squealed.

"Enter it in the state fair?" Mikey suggested.

"How would we even *move* this big head?" snapped Ellen.

Jo Jo didn't say anything. She'd just spotted a flash of green in all the garden green. But this green came with two glowing yellow eyes.

"Uh, I'm going to go get some garden tools," said Jo Jo. "Be right back." She ran over to the small shed at the edge of the garden. Mikey and Ellen kept arguing.

"Over here," whispered the Magic Pickle. He hovered over a rain barrel. "We've got a top-priority, red-alert problem."

"You *think*?!" said Jo Jo. "Look at what your Grow Forth and Conquer did to my homework assignment!"

"Looks like grade A material to me," said the Magic Pickle. "But that's low priority."

"Maybe to you, but it's my report card!" said Jo Jo. "How am I going to explain this?!"

"Again, low priority," answered the Magic Pickle. "Top priority? The Phantom Carrot has escaped from Capital Dill and is at large. Be on the lookout for a ghostly orange agent of evil."

"I know what a bad carrot looks like,"

Jo Jo reminded MP. "How'd he break out?"

"That's classified," the Magic Pickle replied. If he could blush, he would have.

"Well, why do you think he'd come *here*?" Jo Jo asked.

"He seemed interested in the effects of the Grow Forth and Conquer," the Magic Pickle explained. "I fear that this might be the beginning of a very big headache."

"I'll keep an eye on things in the garden," Jo Jo assured him. "You figure out how to make this head of lettuce look like a normal veggie!"

"I'll put some thought into it," the Magic Pickle said. Then in a flash of green he was gone.

Jo Jo walked back to Ellen and Mikey.

"Well, at the very least, I say we drag Miss Emilyek over here and get that A+ now!" said Mikey.

"Don't you think she'll find this all a little odd?" Ellen asked.

"I think we've got a real problem here," Jo Jo agreed.

Neither of them noticed Mikey. He looked like a buffoon, walking around the humongous base of the huge lettuce plant with his arms spread wide.

"I wonder how big this thing really is?" Mikey struggled. "One . . . two . . . three . . ." He used the length of his outstretched arms, from one set of fingertips to the other, as a crude measuring device, counting from where one fingertip touched on the lettuce

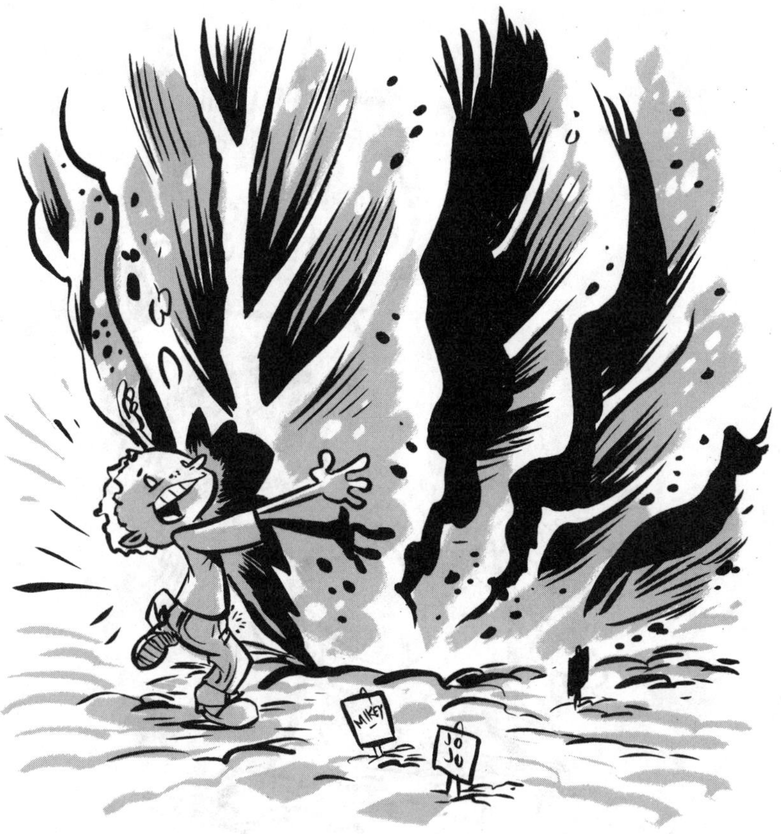
MIKEY
JO
JO

to where the next one touched. Mikey's crazy stretching and counting jiggled the rotten seeds he'd found at the compost heap right out of his pocket. Jo Jo caught a glimpse of the seeds hitting the dirt and gasped.

"MIKEY!" Jo Jo squealed. "What are you doing?!"

"What?" Mikey grunted. "We've got to measure it! This thing's bigger than my house, I bet!"

The earth all around them started to smoke.

"What's happening?" cried Ellen.

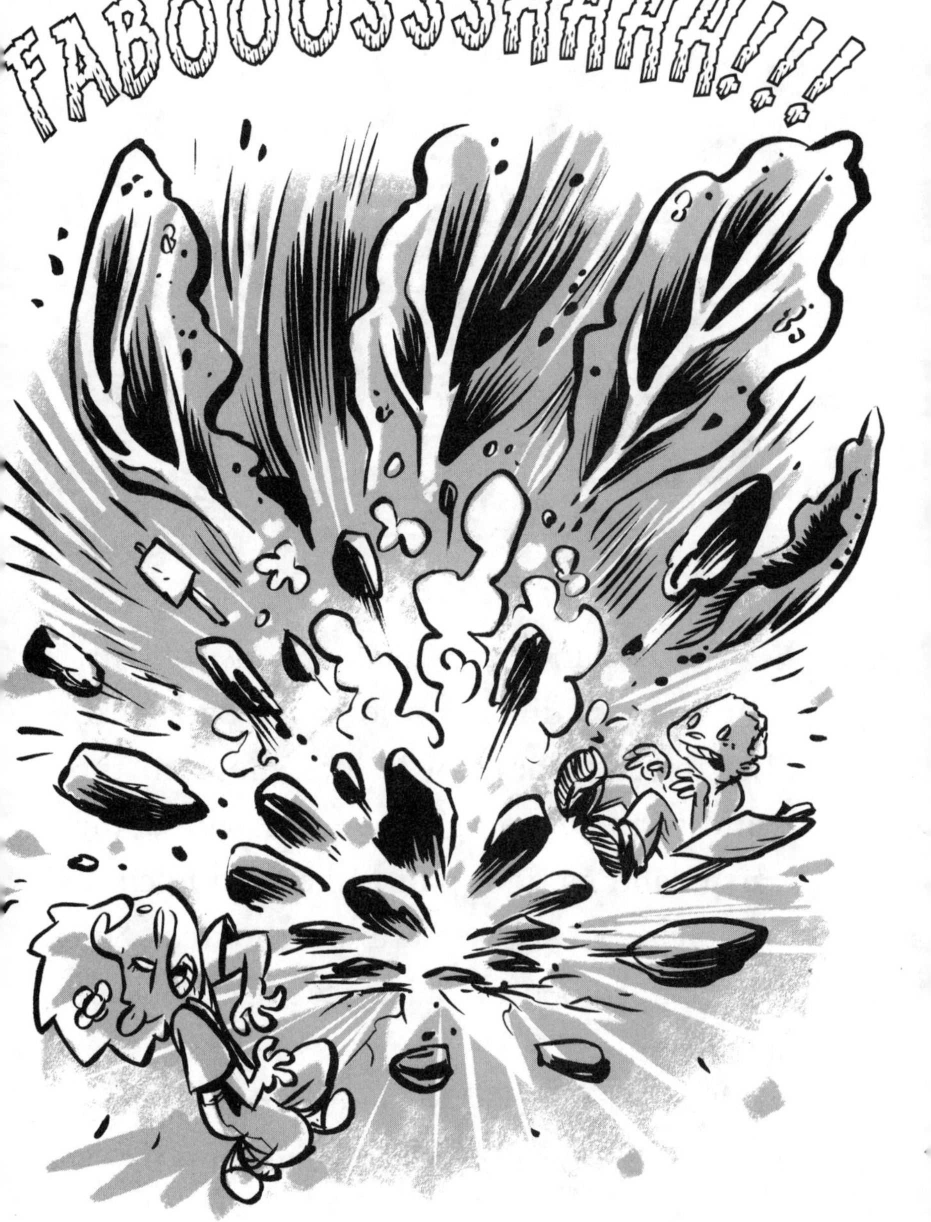
FABOOOSSSHHHH!!!

The ground exploded. Clods of dirt flew in every direction. Jo Jo fell backward. The towering head of lettuce shook in the windstorm. Giant green leaves fell to the earth, landing on top of Mikey and Ellen.

"Help! I can't see!" Ellen shouted. She was trapped beneath a lettuce leaf the size of a parachute.

"Get it off me!" Mikey screamed. He was completely covered by a huge green leaf.

A small leafy globe rose from a smoking hole right where Mikey had dropped his seeds.

"Oh, no!" said Jo Jo.

"BWAHAHAHAHAHA!!!"

Foul and slimy, withered and evil, the ROMAINE GLADIATOR lifted his hands into the air and cackled like a maniac.

"At last, I rise from the dust of bitterness!" cried the Romaine Gladiator. "The world will be *mine at last*!"

"You mean *ours*," another voice chuckled.

"Wha—?" The Romaine Gladiator scowled. He spun around as a puff of orange mist formed near the huge leafy tower of lettuce.

The Phantom Carrot grinned down at the Romaine Gladiator.

"That's right," the Phantom Carrot laughed. He pointed to Jo Jo. "I taunted our good pal, ol' Weapon Kosher, into playing a game of checkers with that bratty little girl there, and now here you are!"

"You're responsible for my rebirth?!" the Romaine Gladiator gasped.

"In a roundabout way," the Phantom Carrot chuckled. "You're just a happy accident. I really just wanted to see how *big* an army the Grow Forth and Conquer would make!"

"But how did you escape?!" Jo Jo screamed.

"Same way you got the grow juice, kiddo," the Phantom Carrot laughed. "Your briny pal is a sucker for a game of checkers."

"I'm also a sucker for a good fight!"

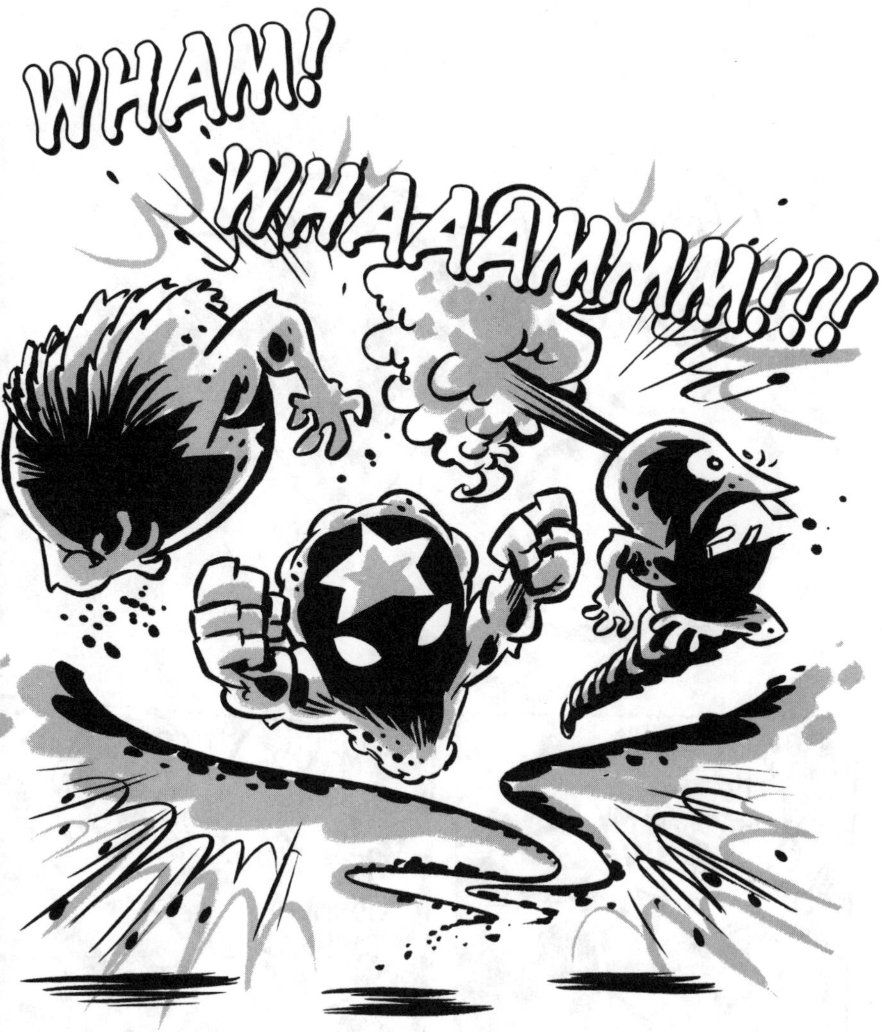
WHAM!
WHAAAAMMM!!!!

The Romaine Gladiator and the Phantom Carrot flew through the air, smacked by two incredibly edible fists.

Green fists.

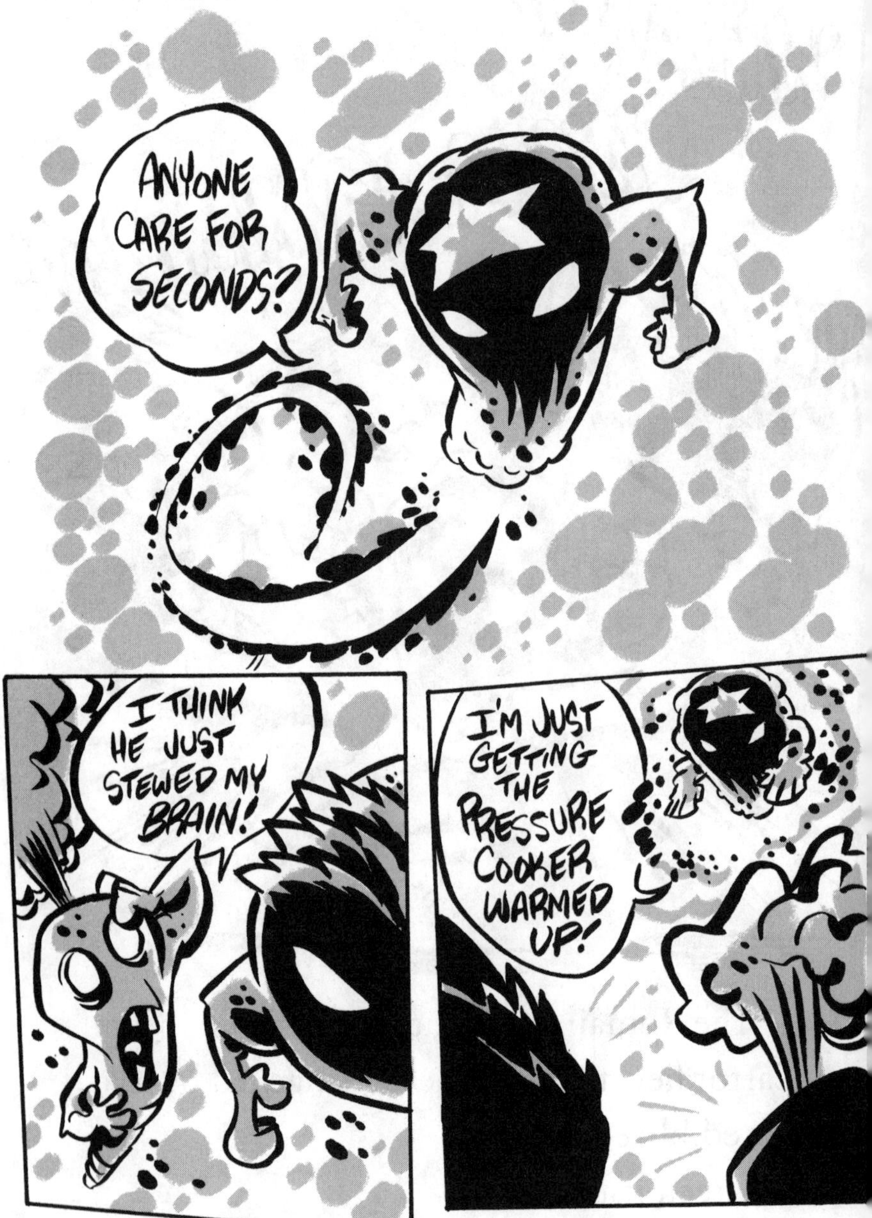
ANYONE CARE FOR SECONDS?
I THINK HE JUST STEWED MY BRAIN!
I'M JUST GETTING THE PRESSURE COOKER WARMED UP!

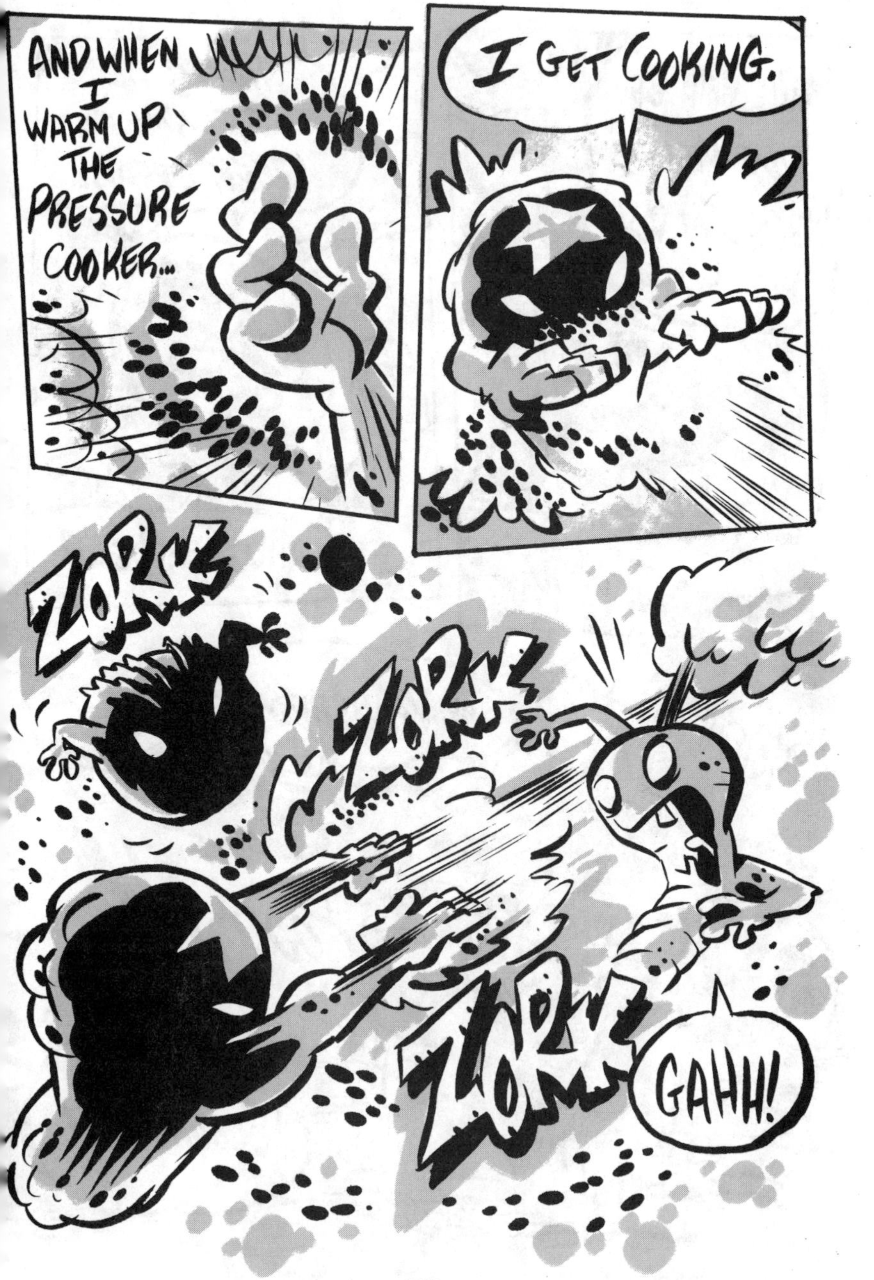
AND WHEN I WARM UP THE PRESSURE COOKER...
I GET COOKING.
ZORK
ZORK
ZORK
GAHH!

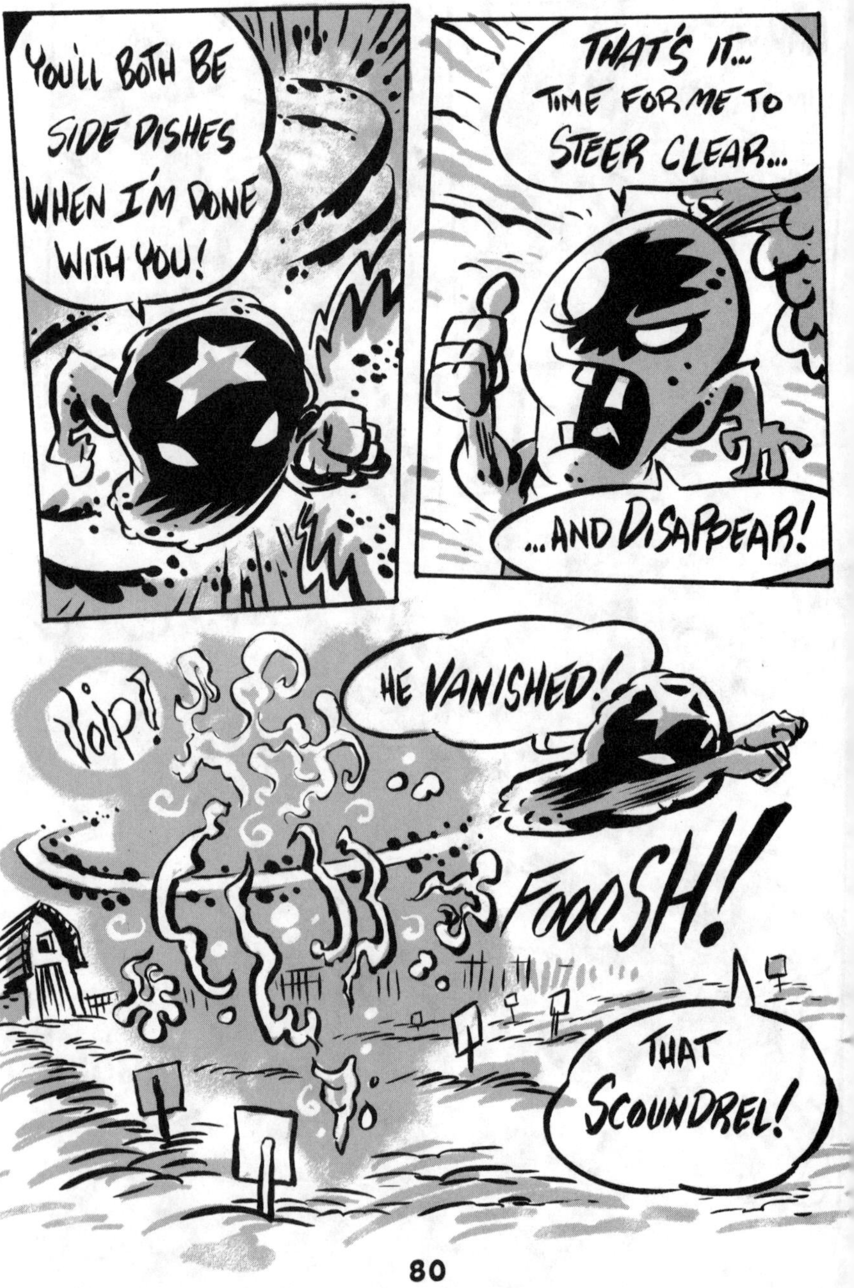
YOU'LL BOTH BE SIDE DISHES WHEN I'M DONE WITH YOU!
THAT'S IT... TIME FOR ME TO STEER CLEAR...
...AND DISAPPEAR!
VOIP!
HE VANISHED!
FOOOSH!
THAT SCOUNDREL!

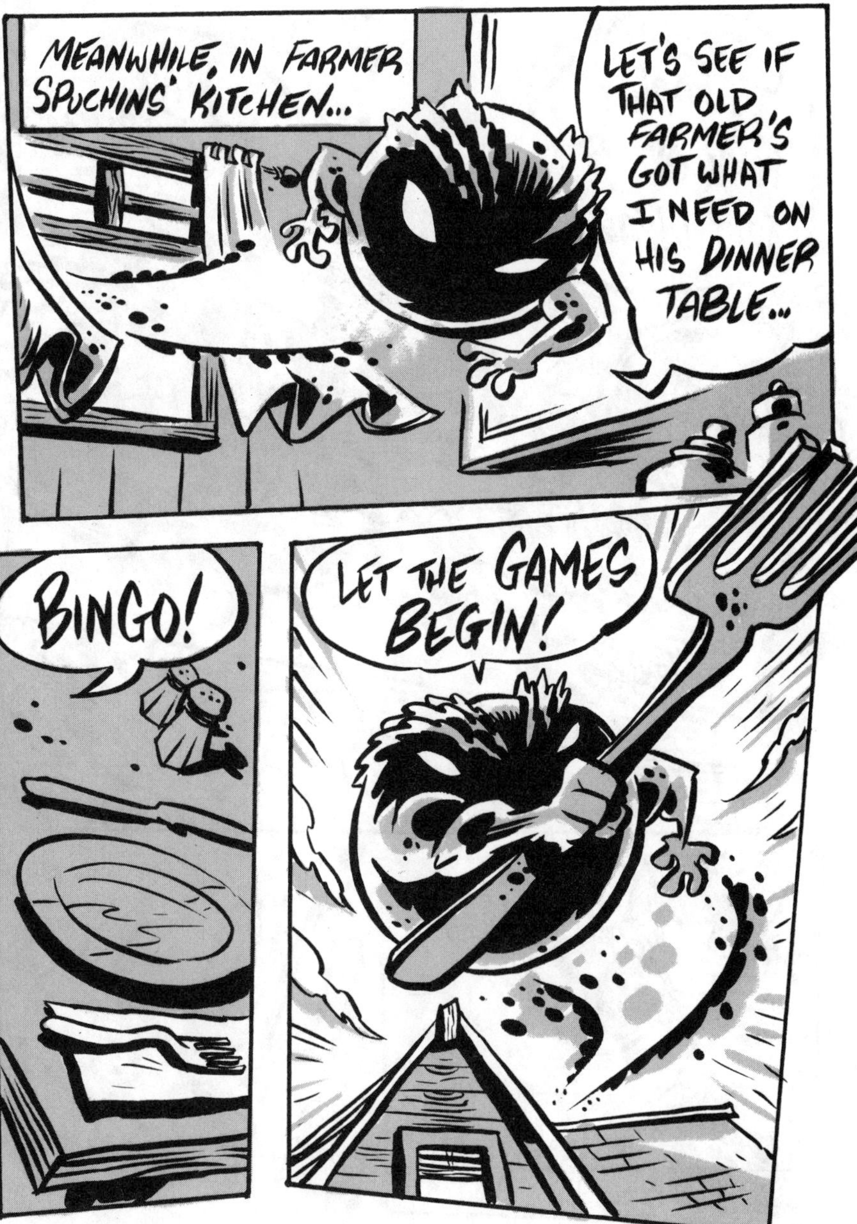
MEANWHILE, IN FARMER SPUCHINS' KITCHEN...
LET'S SEE IF THAT OLD FARMER'S GOT WHAT I NEED ON HIS DINNER TABLE...
BINGO!
LET THE GAMES BEGIN!

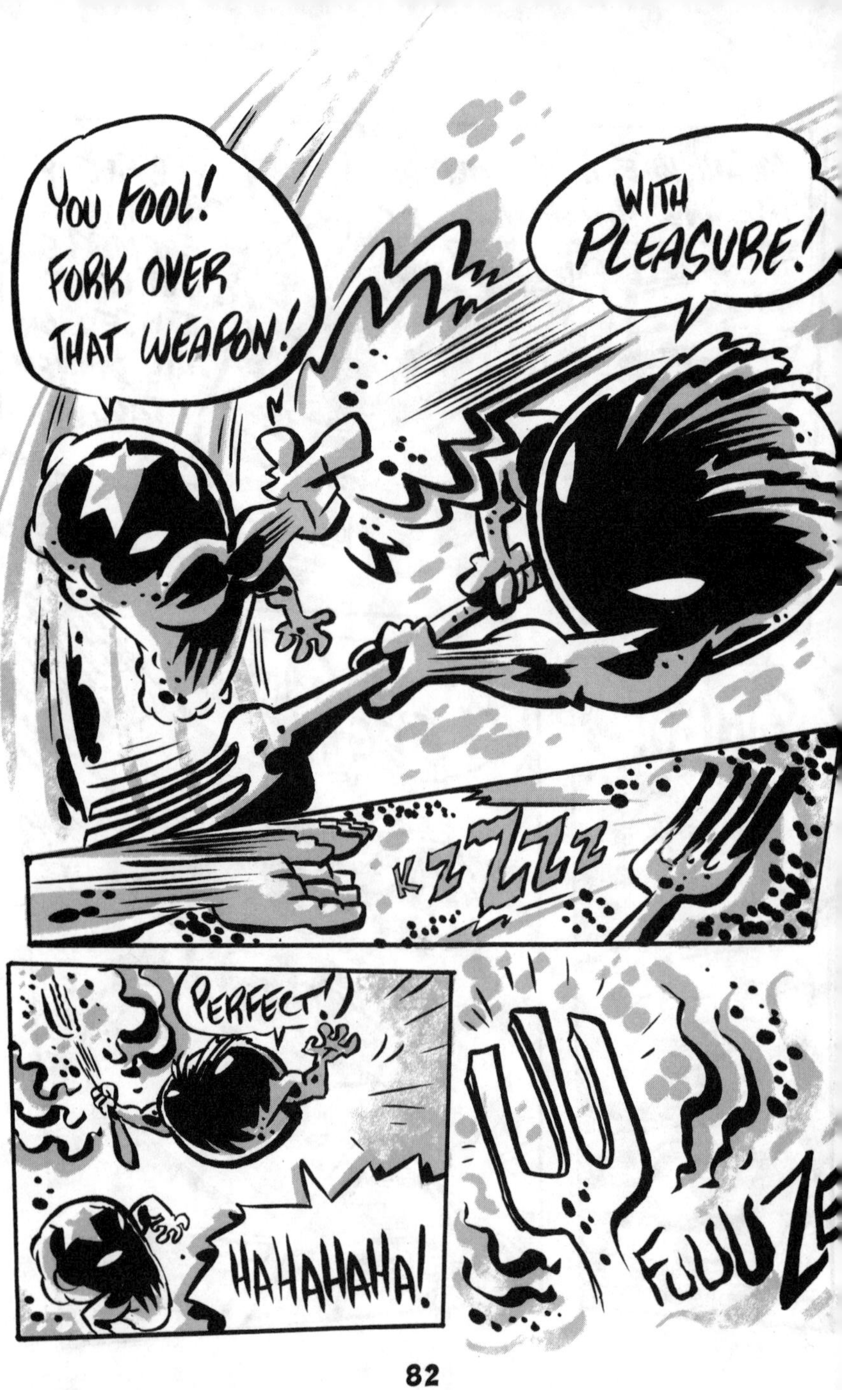
YOU FOOL! FORK OVER THAT WEAPON!
WITH PLEASURE!
KZZZZZ
PERFECT!
HAHAHAHA!
FUUUZE

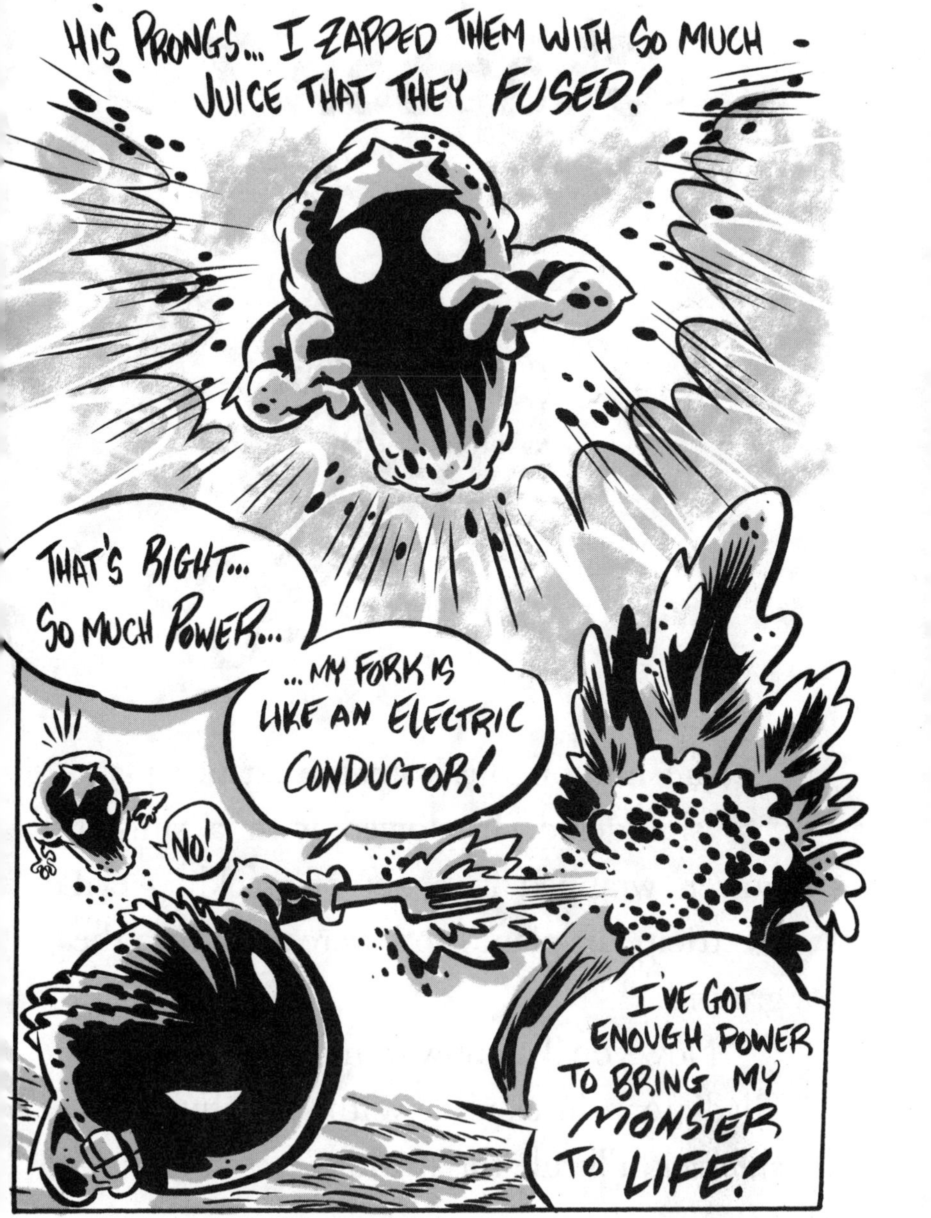
HIS PRONGS... I ZAPPED THEM WITH SO MUCH JUICE THAT THEY FUSED!
THAT'S RIGHT... SO MUCH POWER...
... MY FORK IS LIKE AN ELECTRIC CONDUCTOR!
NO!
I'VE GOT ENOUGH POWER TO BRING MY MONSTER TO LIFE!

Chapter 7

The humongous romaine lettuce plant shuddered. It glowed with a sinister power, wrapped in a net of crackling evil electricity. Its giant roots were torn from the ground.

"Now you'll all bow to me!" the Romaine Gladiator shrieked. "With my five-story sidekick, I'll rule the world!"

"You tell 'em!" said the Phantom Carrot, who had suddenly reappeared.

"You'll rule a cell in the freezer section of Capital Dill, right next to the rest of your Brotherhood of Evil Produce flunkies!" the Magic Pickle replied. He flew around, unable to get a clear shot at the Romaine Gladiator. The giant vegetable beast blocked his path with its broad, huge leaves.

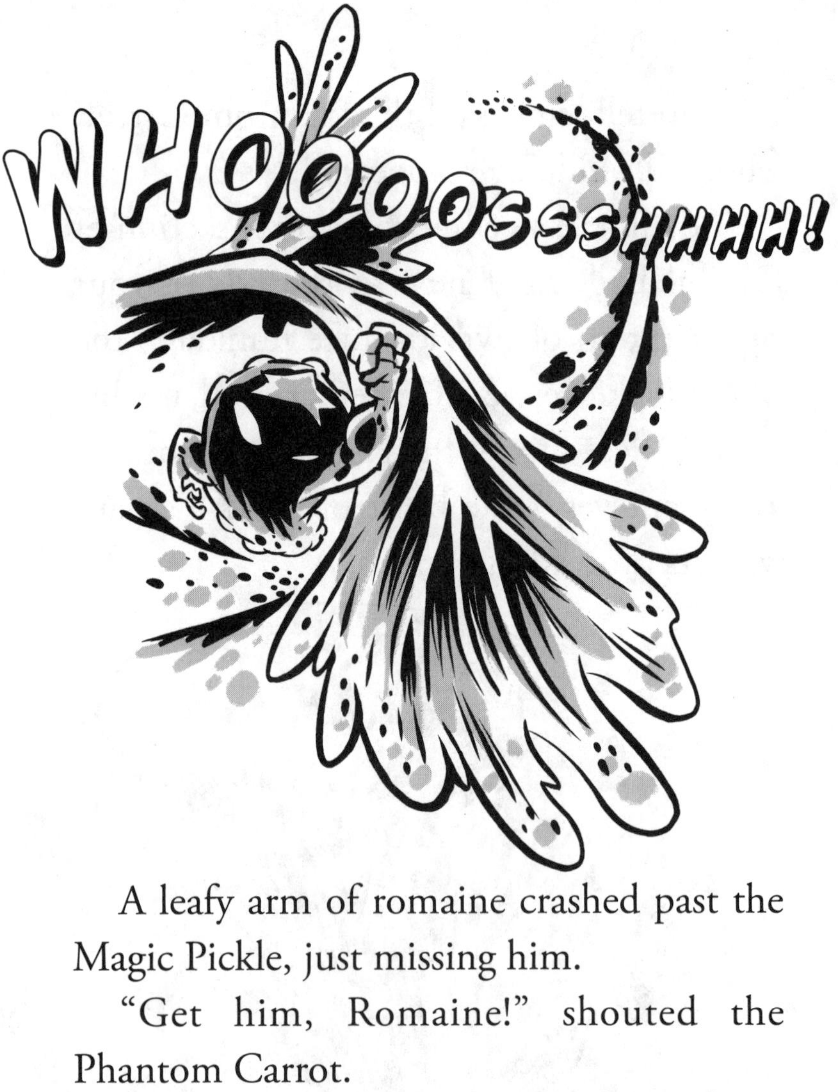
WHOOOOOSSSHHHH!

A leafy arm of romaine crashed past the Magic Pickle, just missing him.

"Get him, Romaine!" shouted the Phantom Carrot.

"What's going on out there?!" cried Ellen, her voice muffled beneath the fallen lettuce leaf.

"Don't worry. I'll get you to safety!" answered Jo Jo. She grabbed the two big leafy blankets that covered Ellen and Mikey and dragged them toward the shed. It was perfect, actually: The big leaves acted like sacks, not letting Ellen and Mikey out to see the strangeness flying all around them. What would they think?! Jo Jo would have to come up with some sort of story later.

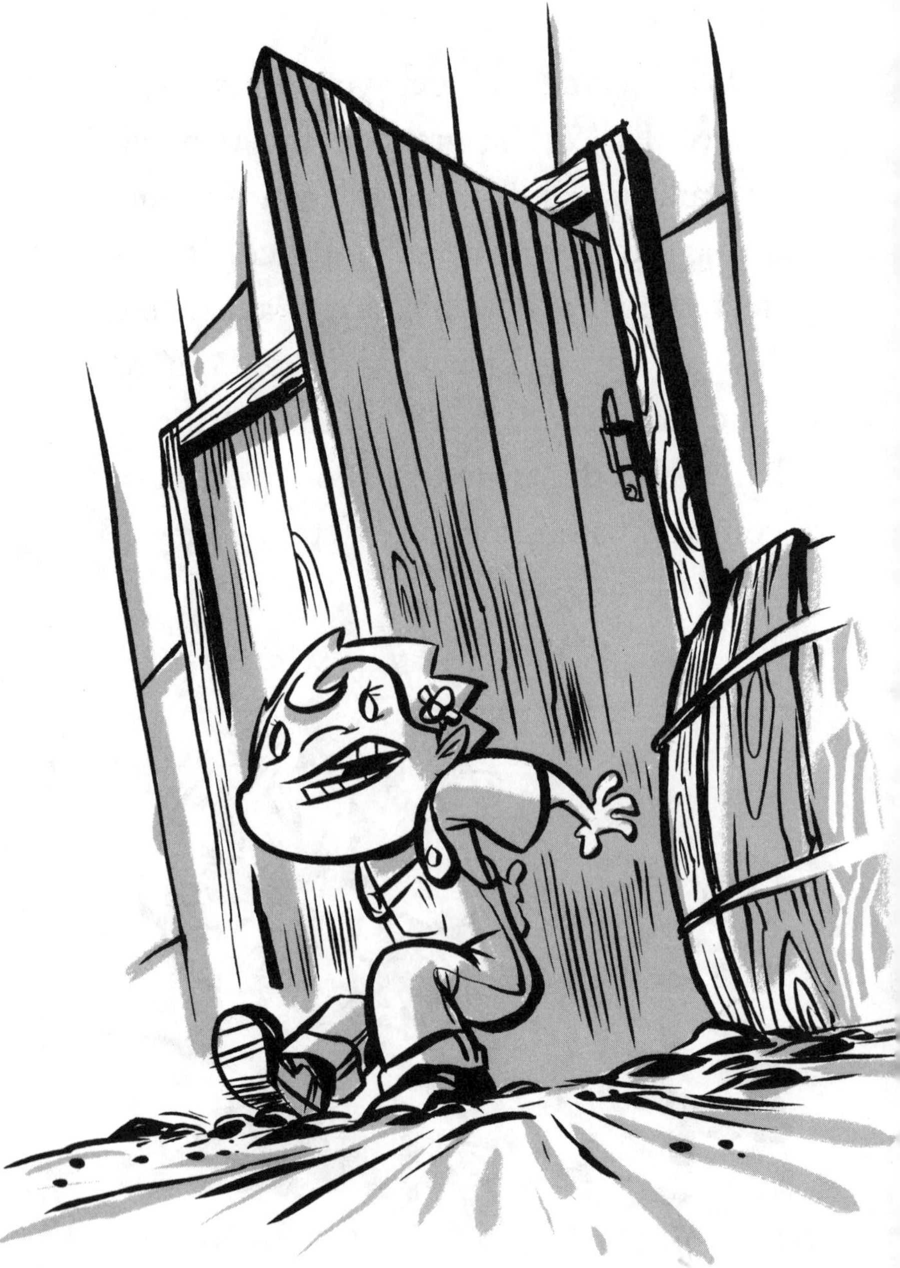

"I can't even see my face!" Mikey whimpered.

"You typically can't see your face unless you're looking in a mirror, Mikey," Jo Jo reminded him. "I'm sure you're fine."

"Oh, yeah," Mikey chuckled. "Right."

Jo Jo flung the leafy sacks into the shed and slammed the door shut behind her.

"I'll be right back!" Jo Jo promised.

"But—!" called Ellen. The rest of her sentence was cut off by the whoosh of the veggie leaf battle.

Chapter 8

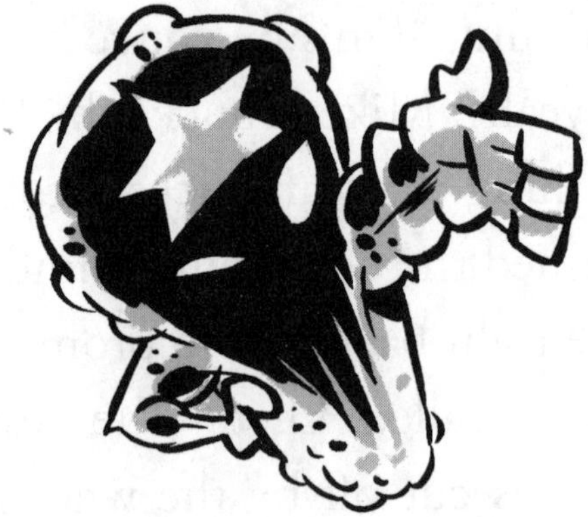

KKLAAAAANNGG!!!

The Magic Pickle swerved in midair.

The Romaine Gladiator's three-pronged fork struck the metal siding of the shed. Missed!

"You've once again underestimated our power," the Romaine Gladiator bellowed.

"I've risen again, and soon I'll release the entire Brotherhood of Evil Produce from your Deep Freeze at Capital Dill. The world will be OURS!"

"Over my bumpy pickled body," the Magic Pickle promised. "You'll never make it past the fence of this small-time garden, you mean ball of leafy greens!"

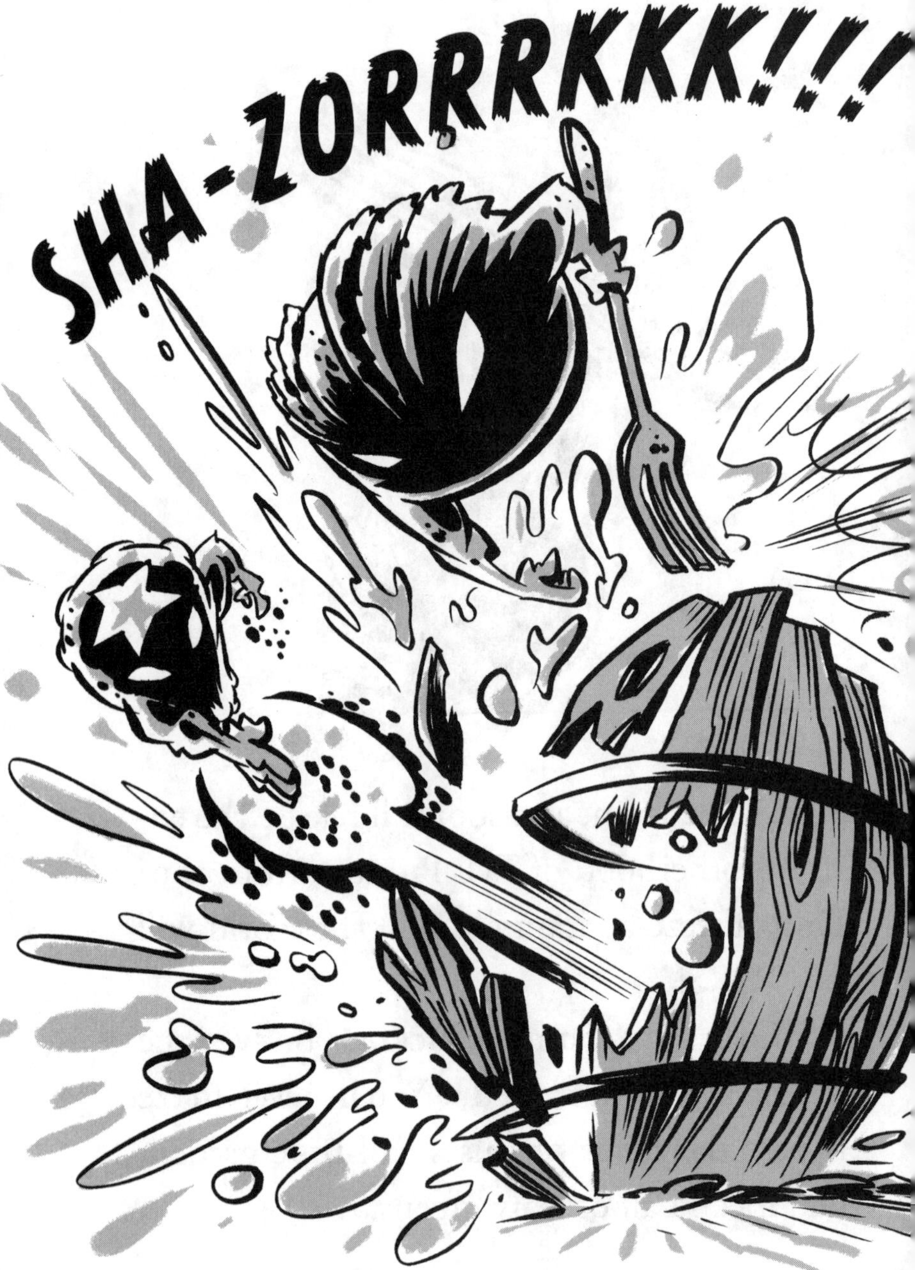
SHA-ZORRRRKKK!!!

The Magic Pickle fired a bolt of luminescent green energy from his fingertips. It missed the Romaine Gladiator by an inch and blew a hole in a big wooden rain barrel near the barn. Wood splinters and water droplets showered down on the garden like rain.

"Time for me to make another exit," said the Phantom Carrot. He disappeared like a ghost into the ground as a blast of green energy just missed him.

"I'm going to relish putting you all behind bars again," the Magic Pickle said with clenched fists.

"Dream on, pickle puss. You've no idea how HUGE our conquest will be!" replied the Romaine Gladiator. "We'll overtake the heartland of America, holding the produce from the nation's farms as hostage. With no food, the humans of the world will beg us for their very survival!"

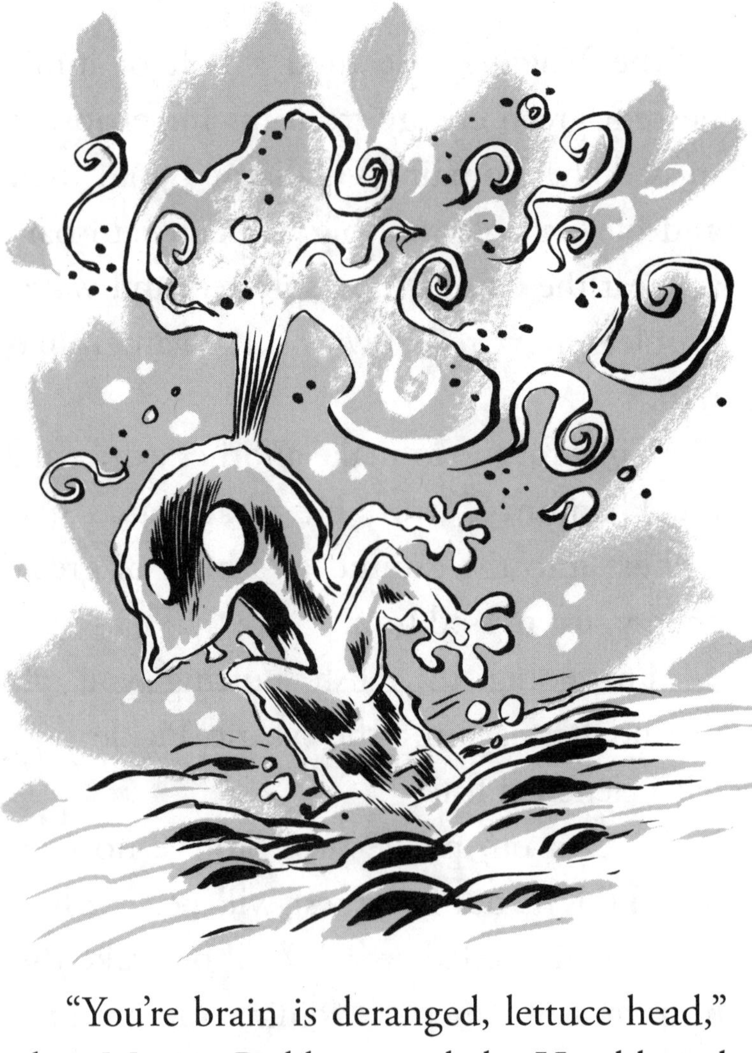

“You’re brain is deranged, lettuce head,” the Magic Pickle growled. He blasted another bolt of energy toward the Romaine Gladiator.

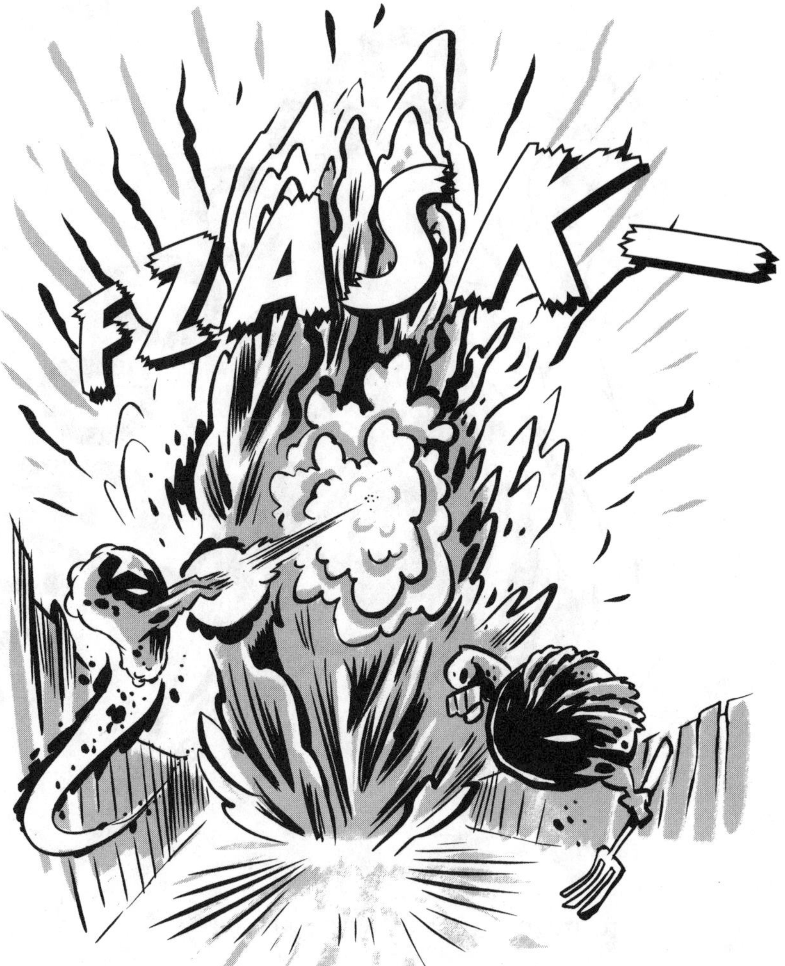
FZASK-

The giant lettuce monster stepped into the Magic Pickle's line of fire at the last second, absorbing the blast of energy. The creature glowed green. And then suddenly . . .

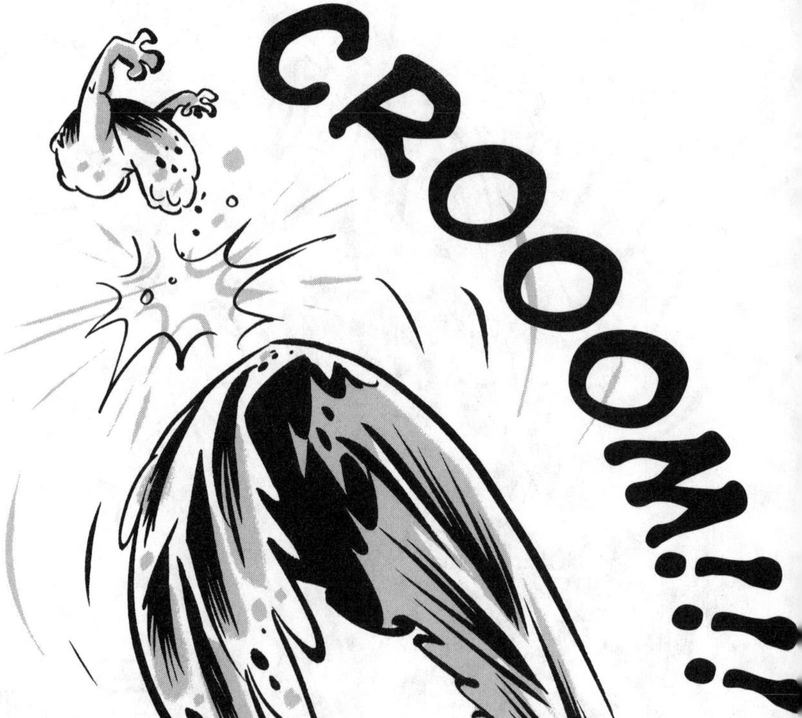
CROOOOM!!!

The giant lettuce monstrosity grew another few feet taller.

"BWAHAHAHAHAHAHAHA!!!" the Romaine Gladiator laughed hysterically. "There's no stopping me this time!"

The monster raised a leafy fist.

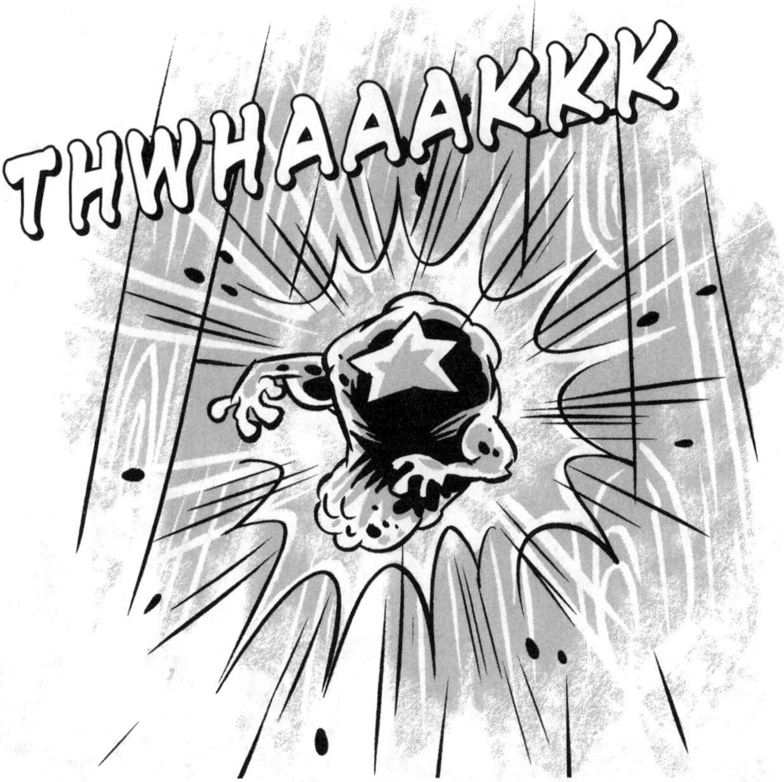
THWHAAAKKK

The gargantuan romaine sent Magic Pickle hurtling backward through the air, smack into the side of the shed.

CLUNK!!!

“Yowww!” Ellen and Mikey yelped from inside.

Magic Pickle slid down the wooden wall of the shed like a limp pillow.

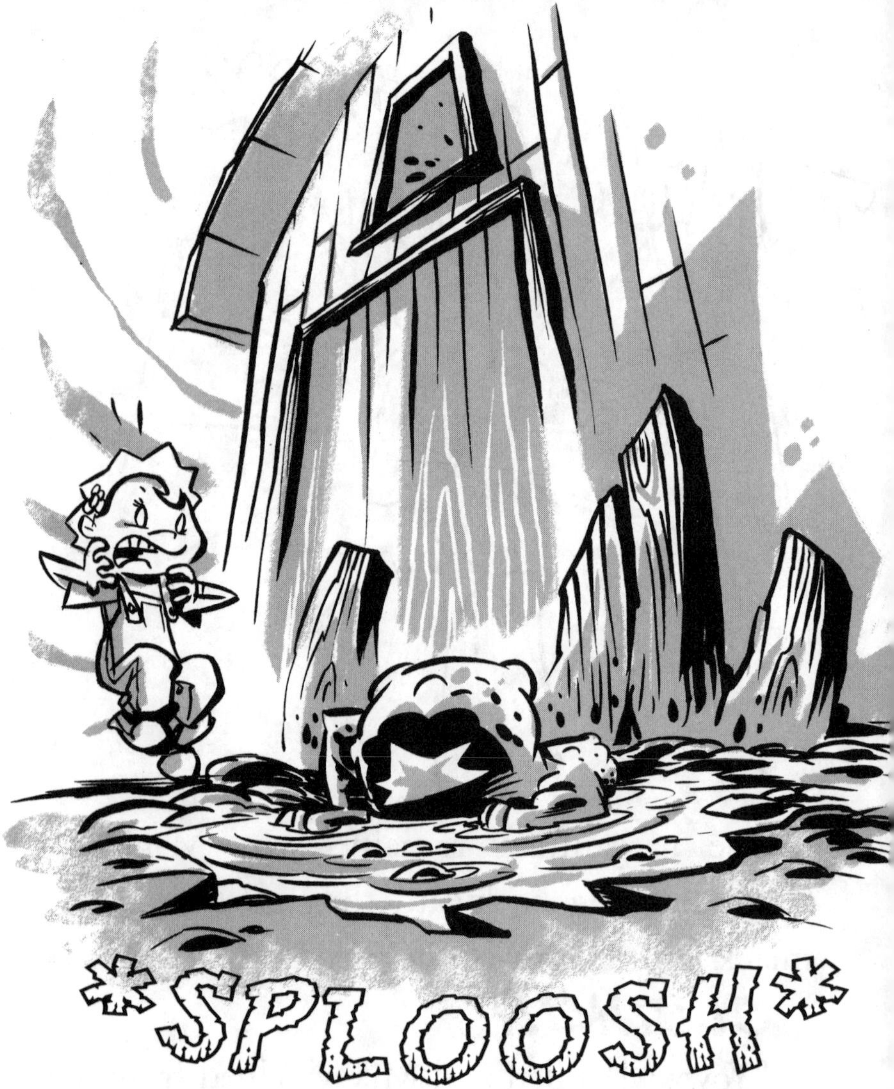
SPLOOSH

The super dill slumped into a muddy puddle, all that remained of the rainwater barrel he'd accidentally zapped earlier.

"MP!" Jo Jo cried. She raced to his side, lifted up his soggy green body, and dusted him off. "I'm sorry!"

"Sorry . . . for . . . what?" Magic Pickle muttered in a daze. "It wasn't *you* who smacked me. . . ."

"Not that," Jo Jo whispered. "Okay, I'm sorry you got hit, even if it wasn't me, but that's not what I'm talking about. I'm sorry I tricked you out of the Grow Forth and Conquer! This is all my fault."

"I . . . blame . . ." Magic Pickle moaned. ". . . myself. If only . . . I was . . . a better checkers player . . ."

"Either way, I'm sorry," said Jo Jo. "But now we've got a bigger problem. A SERIOUSLY bigger problem!"

Jo Jo and the Magic Pickle looked up as the gargantuan green monster flexed his frilly frawns. The Romaine Gladiator floated around the giant lettuce, spinning

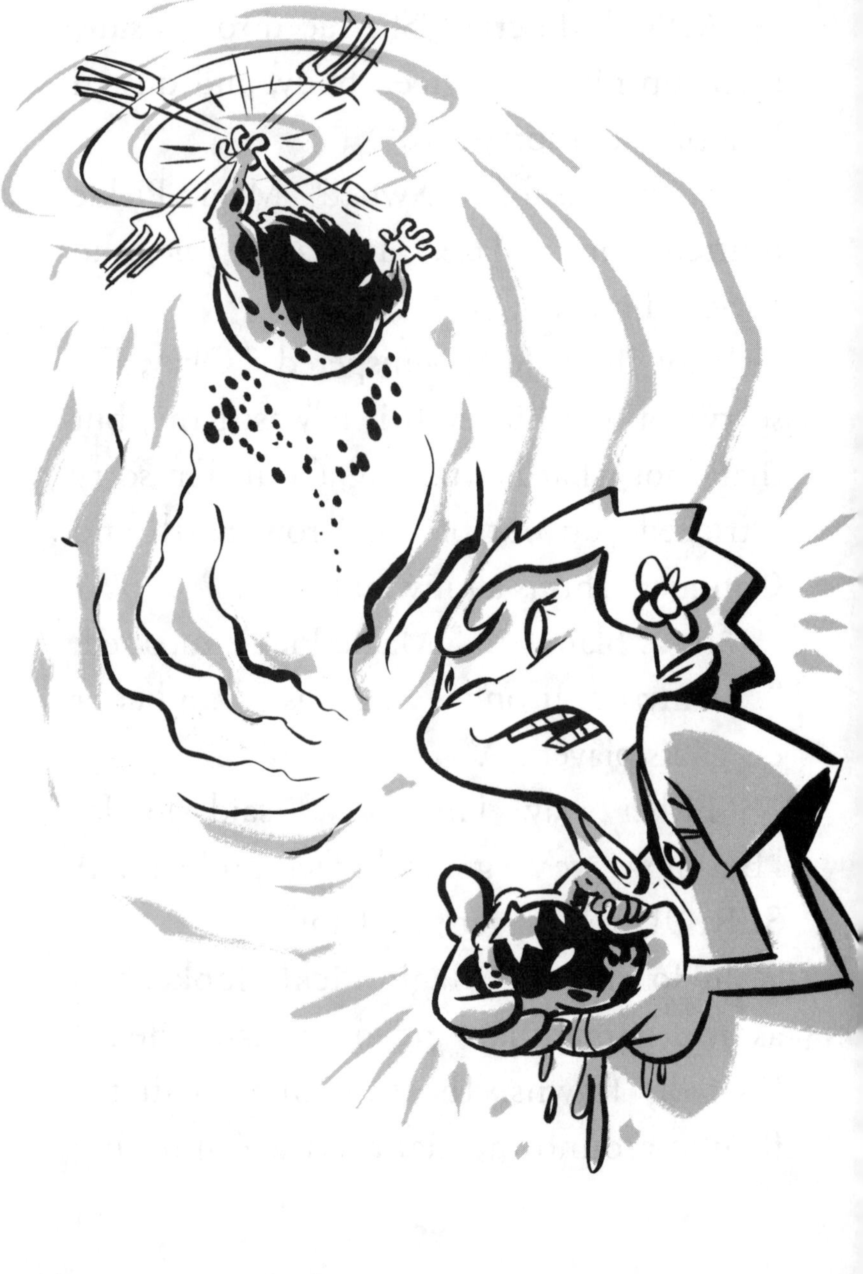

his fork in the air like a marching band baton.

"BWAHAHAHAHA!"

"We've got to stop those leafy beasts!" Jo Jo squinted.

"There's . . . only one . . . way." The Magic Pickle was so dizzy he could barely speak.

"What? WHAT?" begged Jo Jo. "Tell me! We've got to clean our plate of those whackos!"

"Pet . . . rabbits . . ." the Magic Pickle managed to whisper.

"HUH?!" Jo Jo frowned. "Whaddya mean 'pet rabbits'?! I thought you were completely against the idea of me adopting an animal!"

Magic Pickle groaned and slowly lifted his arm, weakly pointing past Jo Jo. She spun around.

"OH! YES!" she cried.

Right behind Jo Jo, at the edge of the

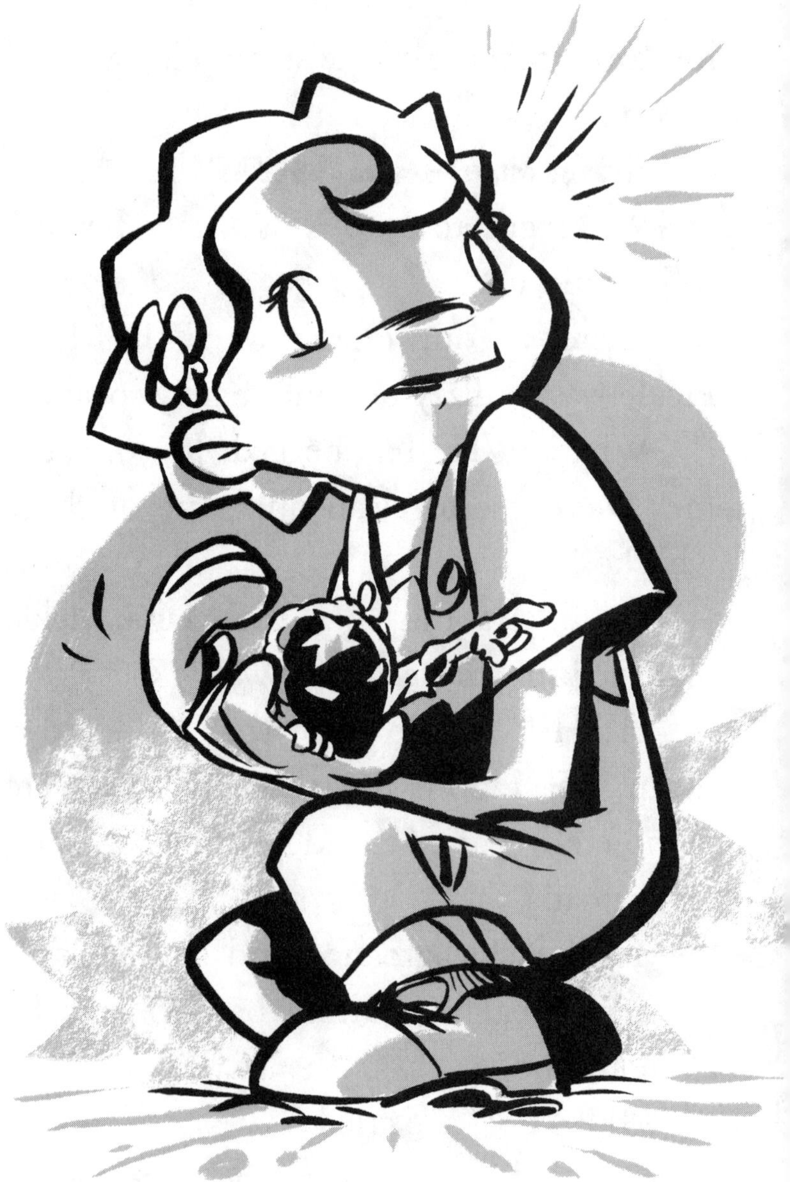

garden, stood the long wooden hutch. The *rabbit* hutch, full of Farmer Spuchins' pet rabbits.

Dozens of them!

"Release the hares," said the Magic Pickle.

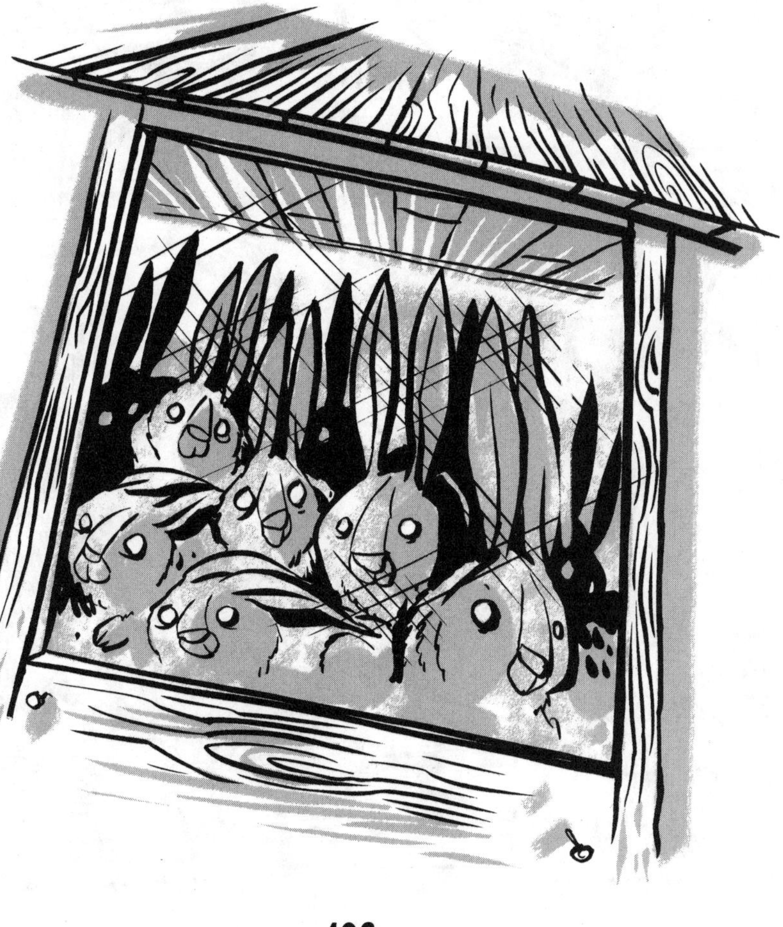

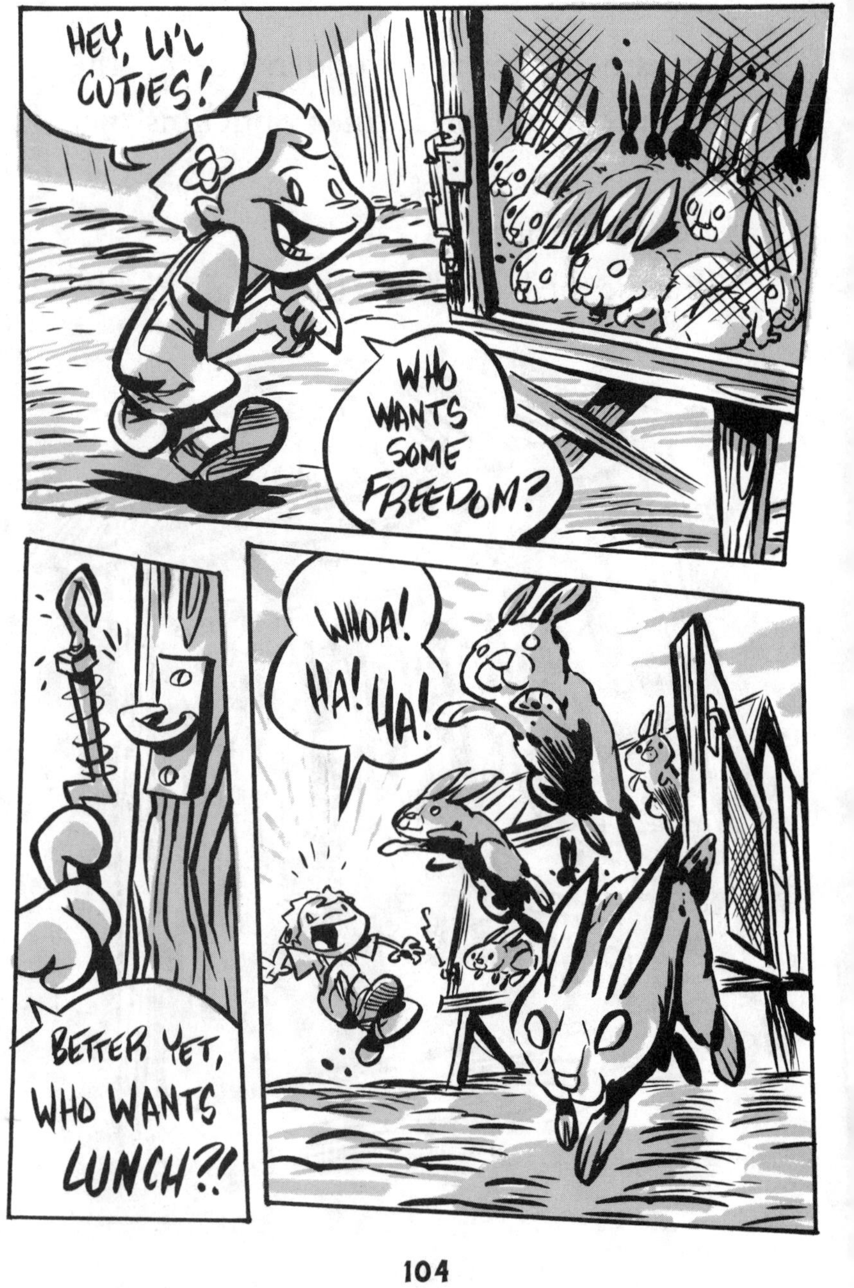
HEY, LI'L CUTIES!
WHO WANTS SOME FREEDOM?
BETTER YET, WHO WANTS LUNCH?!
WHOA! HA! HA!

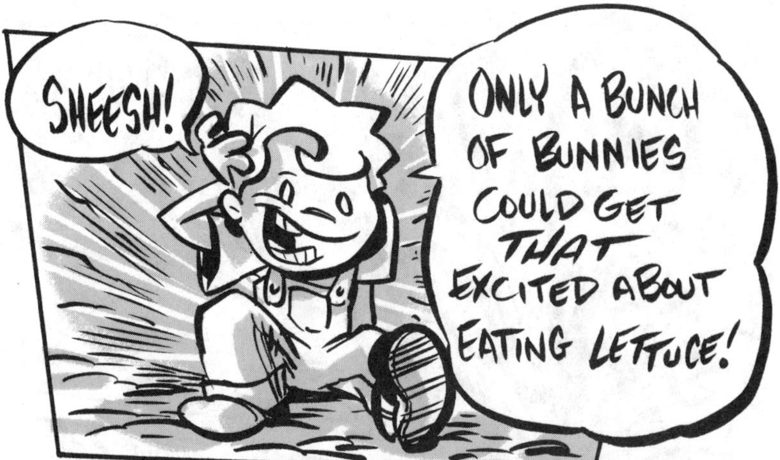
SHEESH!
ONLY A BUNCH OF BUNNIES COULD GET THAT EXCITED ABOUT EATING LETTUCE!

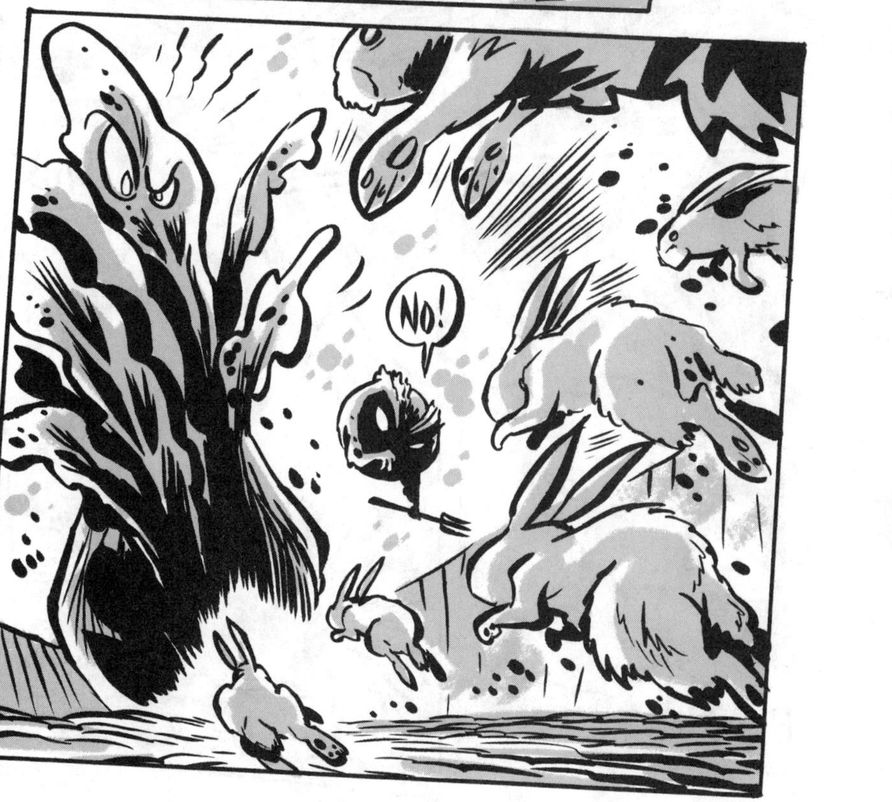
NO!

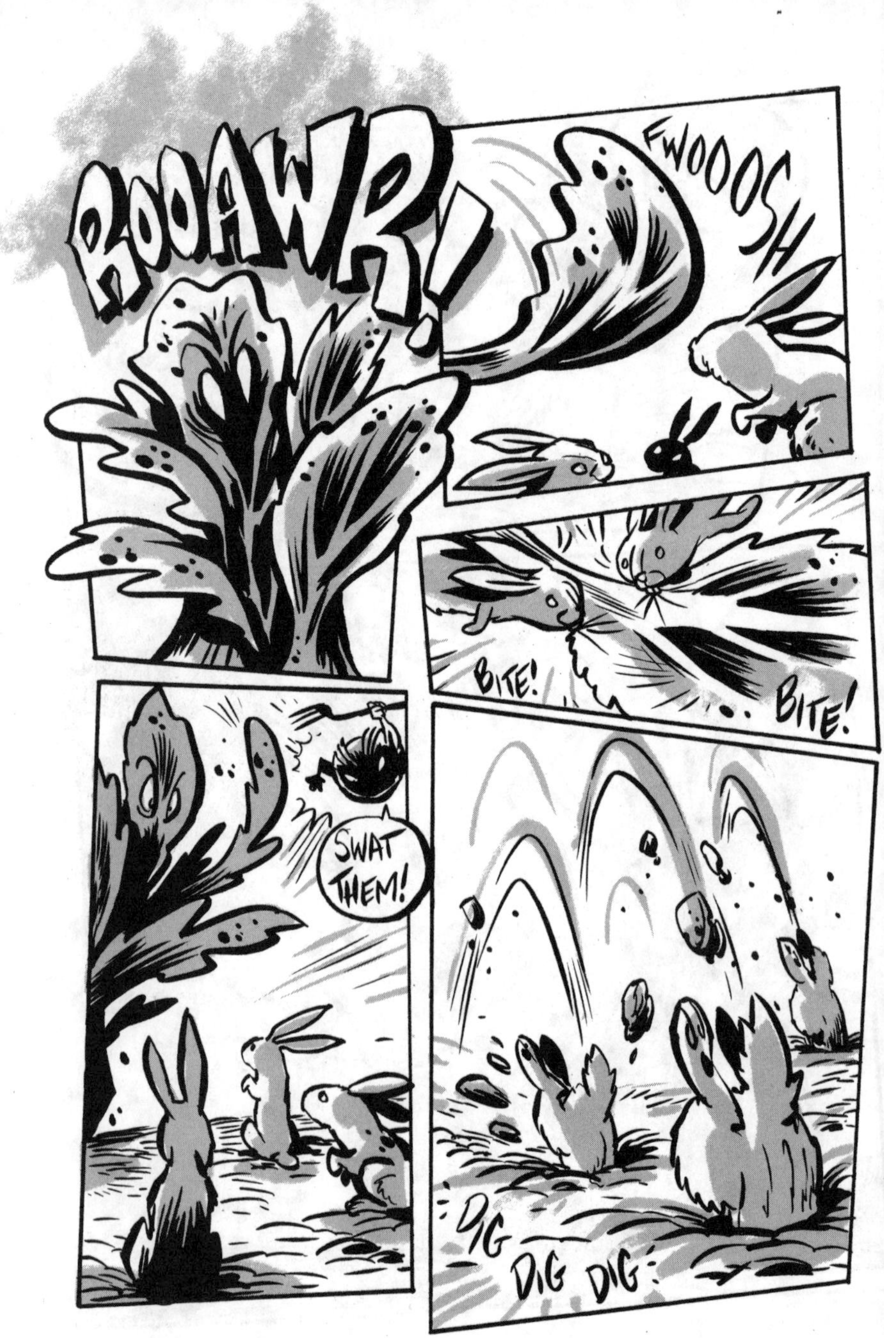
ROOAWR!!
FWOOOSH
BITE!
BITE!
SWAT THEM!
DIG
DIG DIG

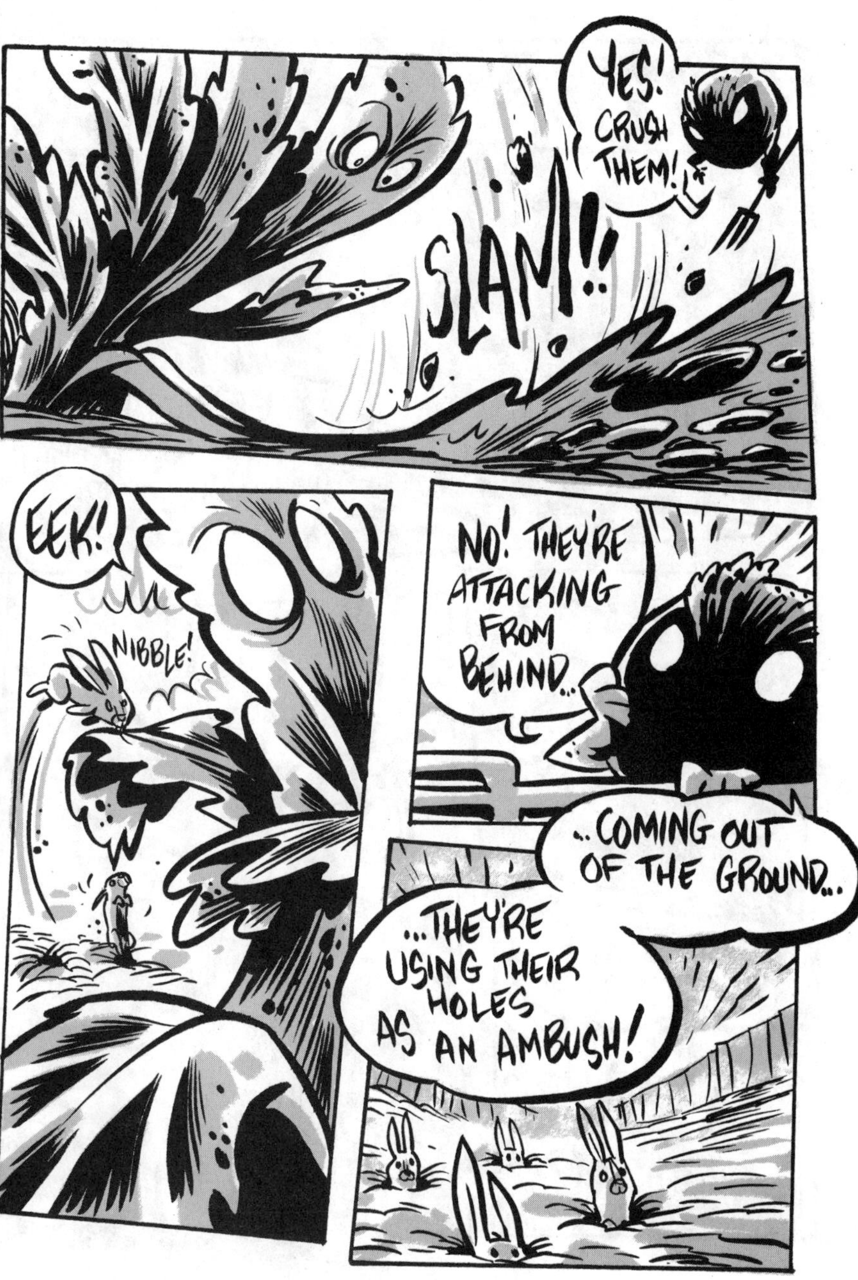
YES! CRUSH THEM!
SLAM!!
EEK!
NIBBLE!
NO! THEY'RE ATTACKING FROM BEHIND...
...COMING OUT OF THE GROUND...
...THEY'RE USING THEIR HOLES AS AN AMBUSH!

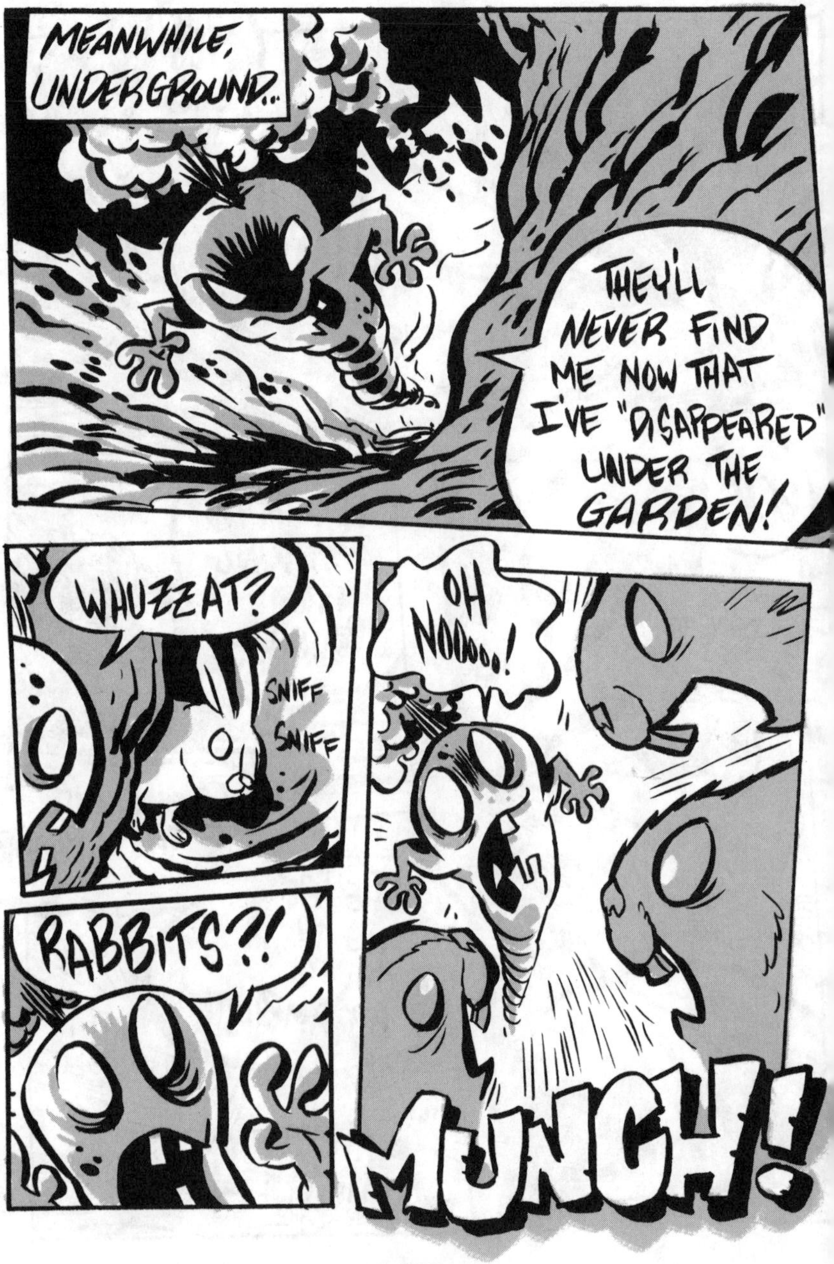
MEANWHILE, UNDERGROUND...
THEY'LL NEVER FIND ME NOW THAT I'VE "DISAPPEARED" UNDER THE GARDEN!
WHUZZAT?
SNIFF
SNIFF
RABBITS?!
OH NOOOO...!
MUNCH!

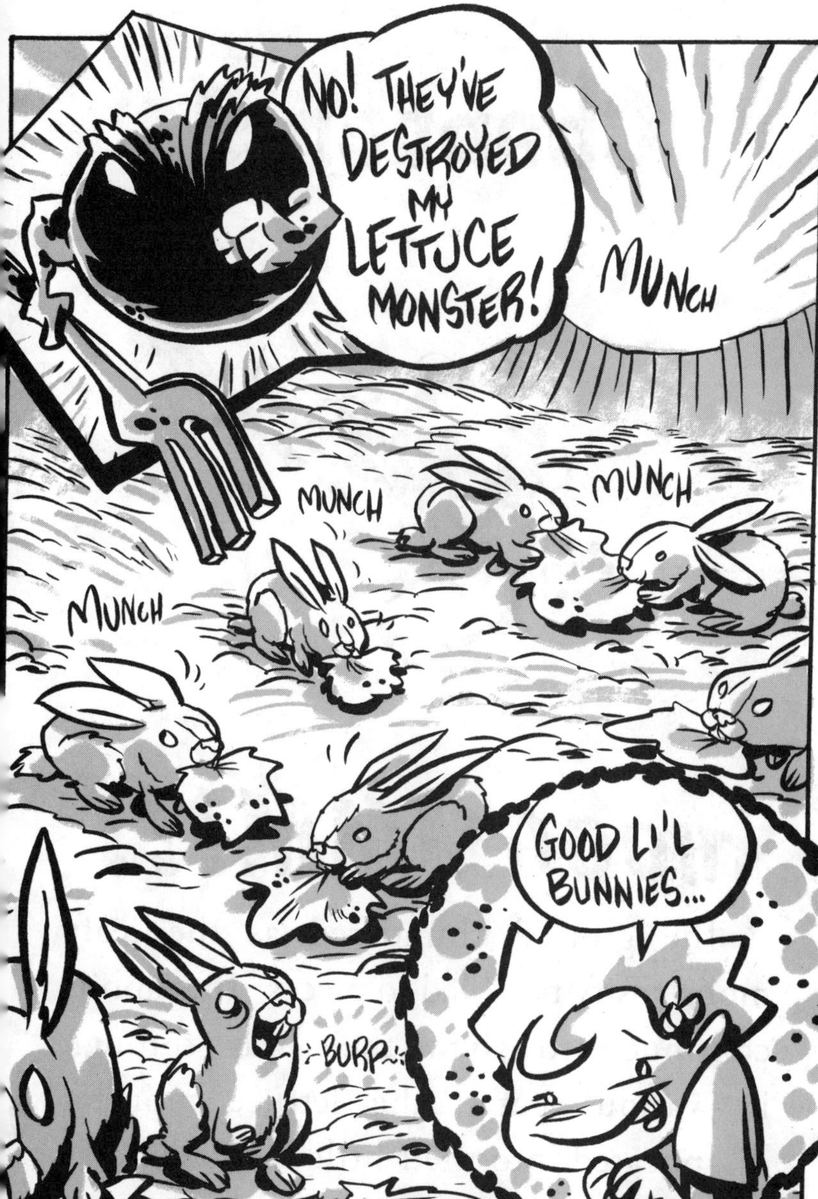
NO! THEY'VE DESTROYED MY LETTUCE MONSTER!
MUNCH
MUNCH
MUNCH
MUNCH
GOOD LI'L BUNNIES...
BURP

Chapter 9

THOOOMMM!!!

The ground thundered as the leafy monstrosity tumbled to pieces. The rabbits continued to chew their way through its various parts; the lettuce monster disappeared into their little furry bellies.

"NOOO!!!" the Romaine Gladiator cried.

"My beautiful green giant! DESTROYED!"

"All *right*!" Jo Jo cheered. She turned to high-five the Magic Pickle.

"Hey, where'd you go?!" Jo Jo frowned.

"Over here!" called the Magic Pickle. "The rabbit rally has given me new strength!" He flew past Jo Jo in a green streak, headed straight for his target.

"You'll pay dearly for this, you vinegar-veined fool," the Romaine Gladiator hissed. He opened his hands and out shot bolts of leafy lettuce like huge nets. The Magic Pickle ducked and swerved, blasting the lettuce nets to bits.

SHZAAAAKKK!

"You know what's funny?" asked the Magic Pickle. "I've been doing some research back at Capital Dill."

"That's HILARIOUS," the Romaine Gladiator growled. He waved his fork in an arc, trying to slash at the Magic Pickle.

"Not *that* part. It's what I've *discovered* that's funny," continued the Magic Pickle. "Apparently, you're an even bigger numb-skull than I originally thought!"

"And how did you come to that mighty conclusion?" snapped the Romaine Gladiator. He tried another slice at the Magic Pickle.

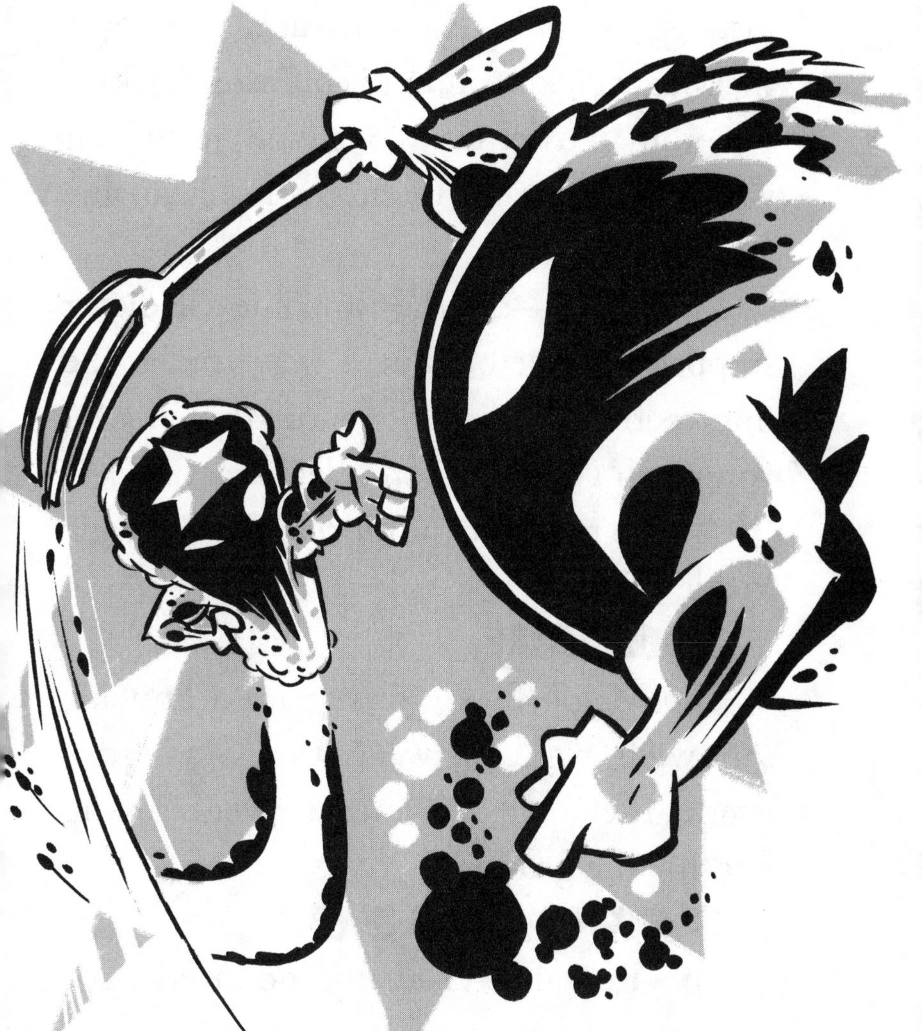

"Well, it seems you're no gladiator, you're just regular old iceberg lettuce," answered the Magic Pickle. "Your big monster sidekick was romaine lettuce, long and leafy, but you hardly live up to the name 'Romaine Gladiator.'"

"Wh-what—?!" The Romaine Gladiator stopped, puzzled. "But I was under the impression . . . I mean, I grew up thinking . . . you mean I'm not *romaine* lettuce . . . ?"

"You're not romaine *anything*," the Magic Pickle roared.

SMACK!

The Magic Pickle served up a knuckle sandwich right between the Gladiator's eyes. The ball of lettuce went flying and hit the ground.

SPROINGGG!

The Romaine Gladiator bounced back into action and spun around to face the Magic Pickle.

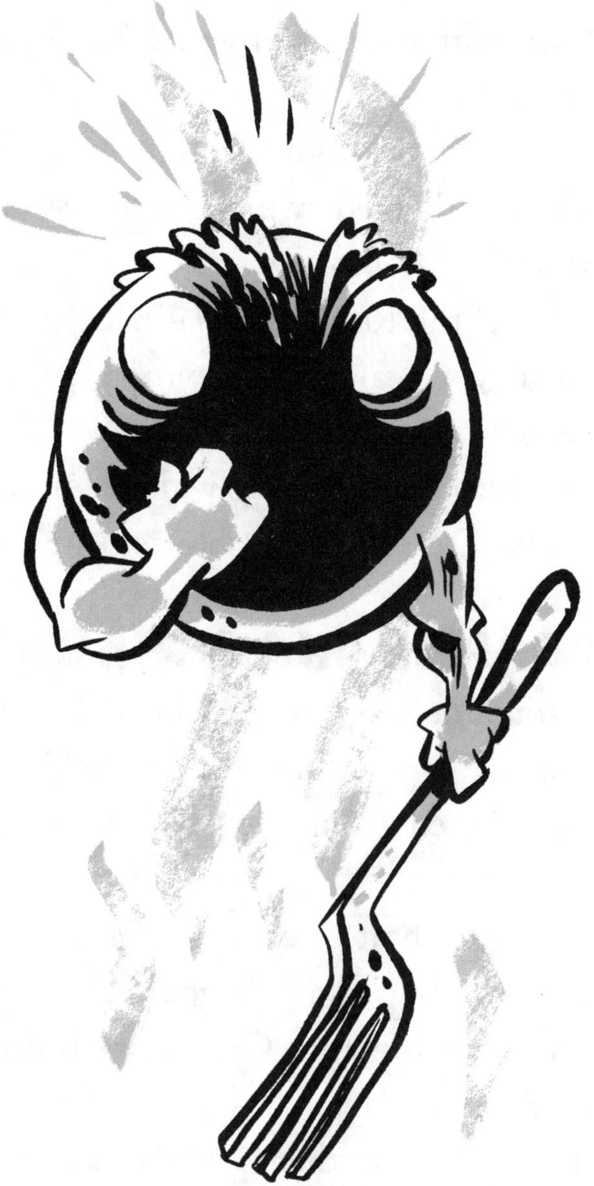

"No matter," he grunted. "You're not so smart yourself."

"How do you figure?" asked the Magic Pickle. He dodged swipes from that razor-sharp fork of doom.

"Well," the Romaine Gladiator sneered, "I hear you can't even win a game of *checkers*."

The Magic Pickle's eyes widened in shock.

"How DARE you?!" shouted the Magic Pickle.

"HAHAHAHAHAHAHA!!!" the Romaine Gladiator cackled. He dead-aimed his fork at the Magic Pickle. Red energy sizzled from the tips of the three prongs.

Bolt after bolt of energy shot out at the Magic Pickle, who dodged at lightning speed. The Romaine Gladiator continued to fire.

The land below them was now a complete

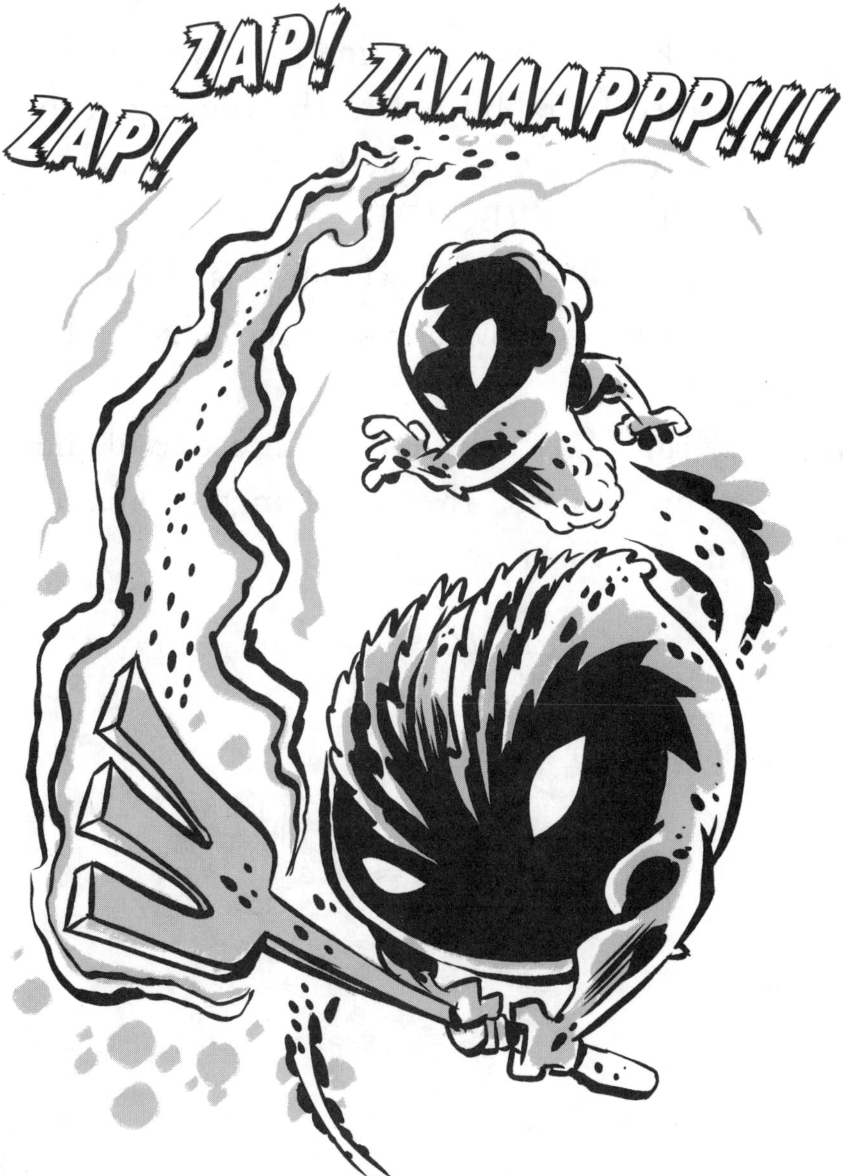
ZAP!
ZAP!
ZAAAAAPPPP!!!

wreck. The class's planting rows were pock-marked by rabbit holes. The whole garden looked like a big checkerboard.

CHECKERBOARD?!!??

Magic Pickle's briny brain began to buzz.

"Time to bow down to the KING!" he said.

The Magic Pickle dove into one of the rabbit holes. The No-Longer-Romaine Gladiator lost track of him.

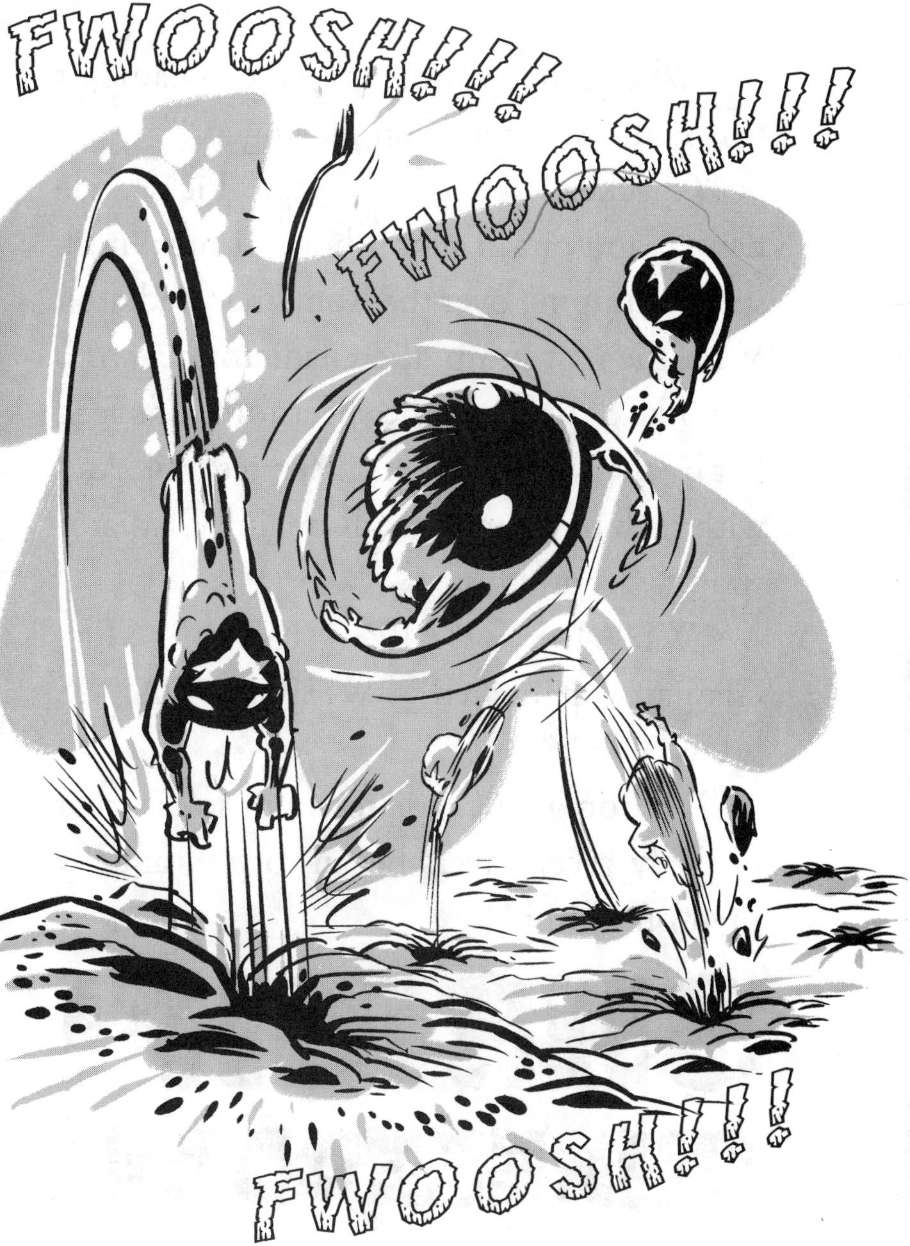
FWOOSH!!!
FWOOSH!!!
FWOOSH!!!

"Whu-huh?" The Romaine Gladiator frowned. "What are you playing at?!"

"Checkers!" cried the Magic Pickle. He flew in and out of rabbit holes at breakneck speed, jumping over the Romaine Gladiator. With the first jump, the Gladiator began to spin like a top from the sheer force of speed left by the Magic Pickle's green jet trail. And with each new jump, the Romaine Gladiator spun faster and faster.

"WHAT'S HAPPENING?!" The Gladiator panicked. "WHICH WAY IS UUUPPP???"

The Romaine Gladiator spun so fast that his leafy green layers began to peel and fly right off of him!

SHRIIIIP! SHREEEDDD!!!

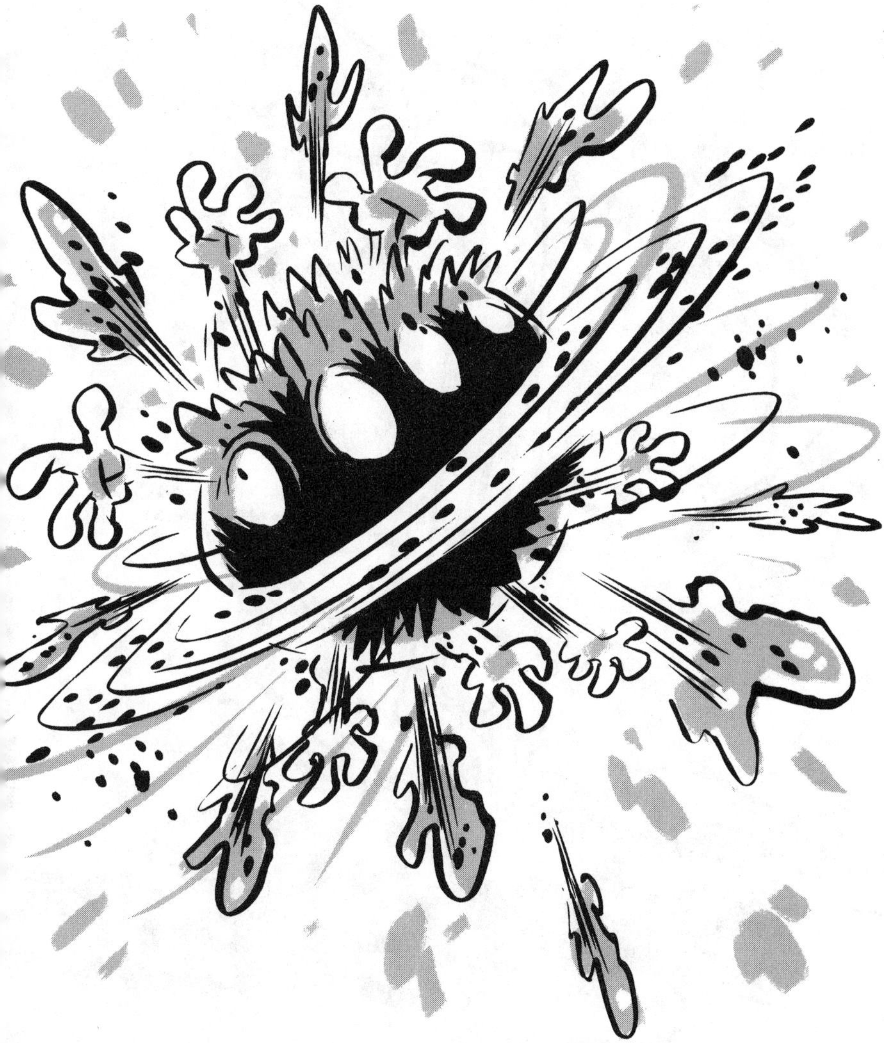

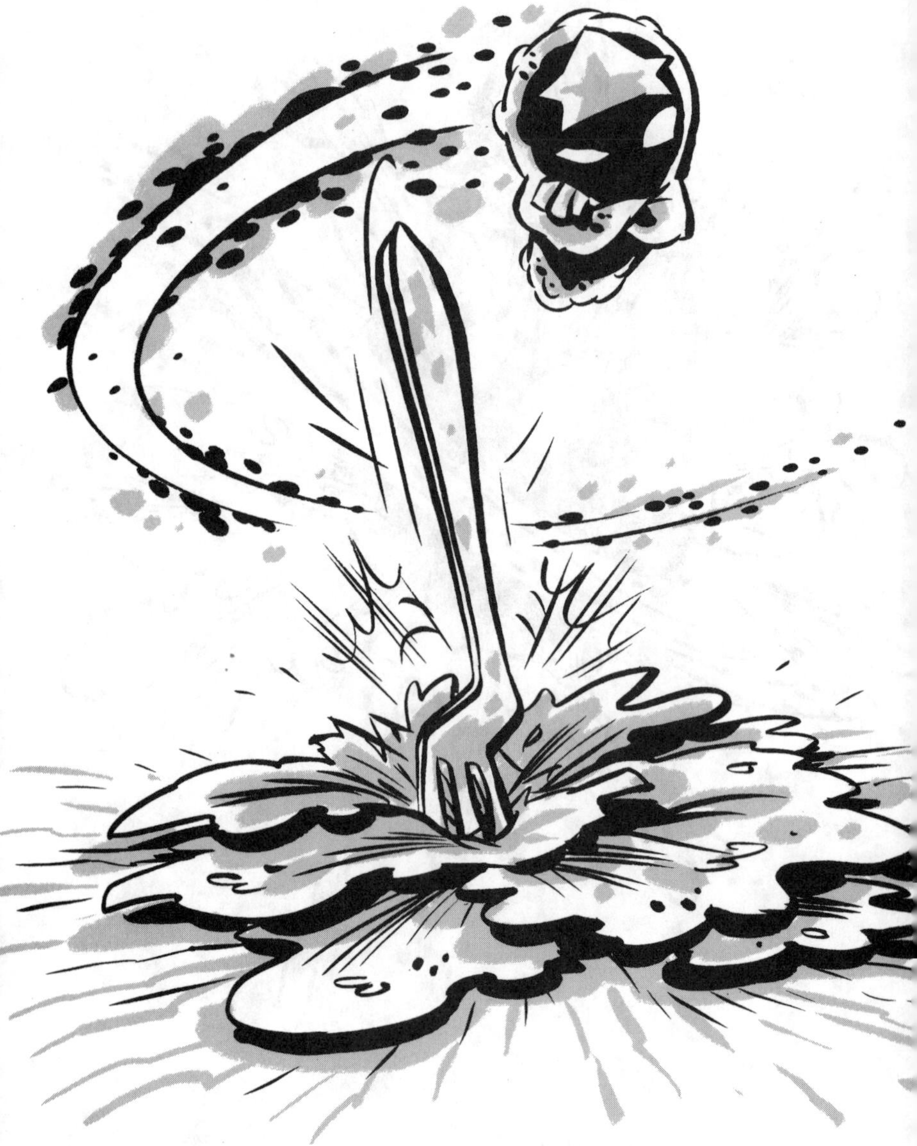

"NOOO!!!" the Gladiator cried, but the cry trailed off into nothing. The Romaine Gladiator had spun so fast he'd shredded himself, leaving nothing but a pile of leafy lettuce leaves on the ground.

SPRONG!

His fork of doom stuck itself into the pile of leafy greens like a meal ready to be eaten.

"Salad, anyone?" said the Magic Pickle.

"HAHA!" Jo Jo laughed with pride. "You served him up GOOD!"

Chapter 10

Jo Jo swung open the shed doors. Light spilled in on the huge leafy lettuce sacks wrapping up Mikey and Ellen. Their bodies were still trapped, but their heads were free.

The Magic Pickle, of course, had disappeared back to Capital Dill to file his report on the defeat of the Romaine Gladiator and the smackdown of The Brotherhood of Evil

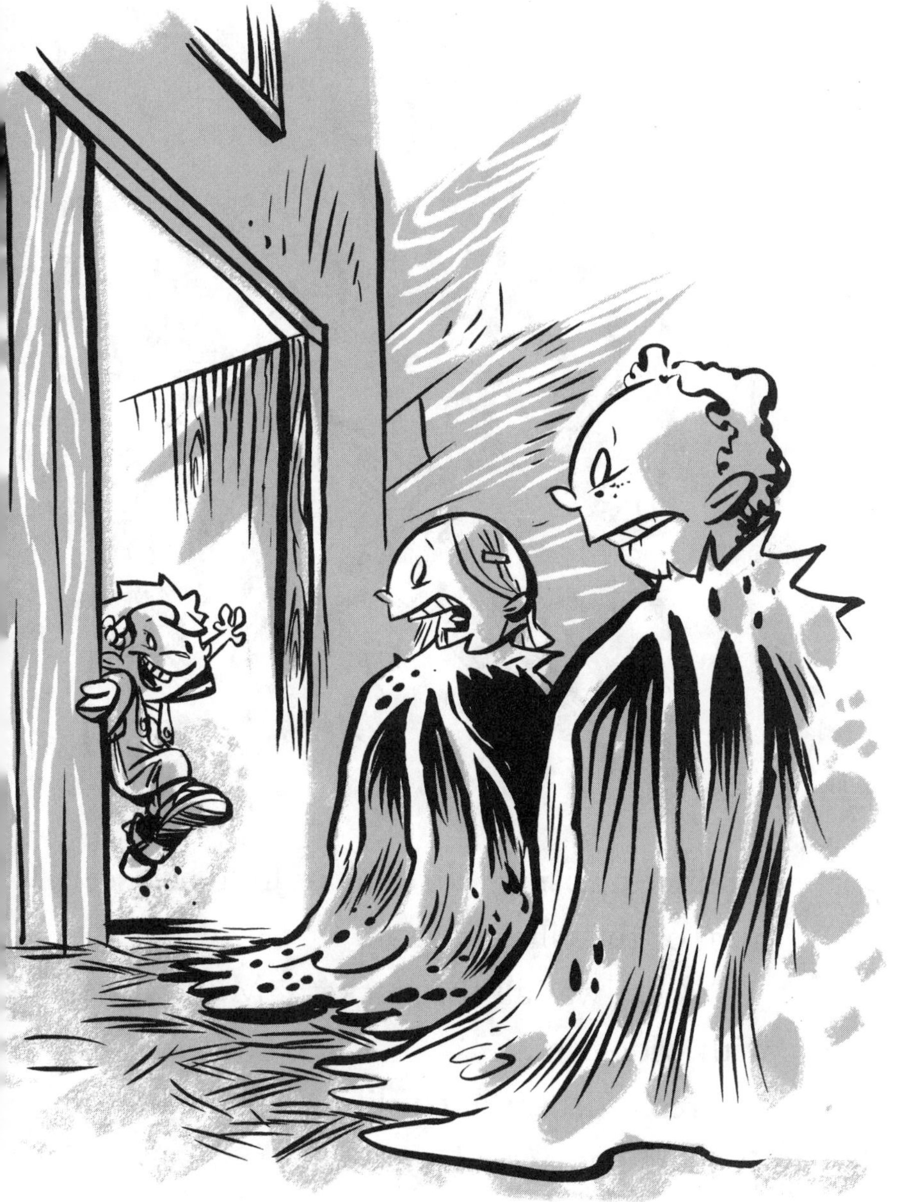

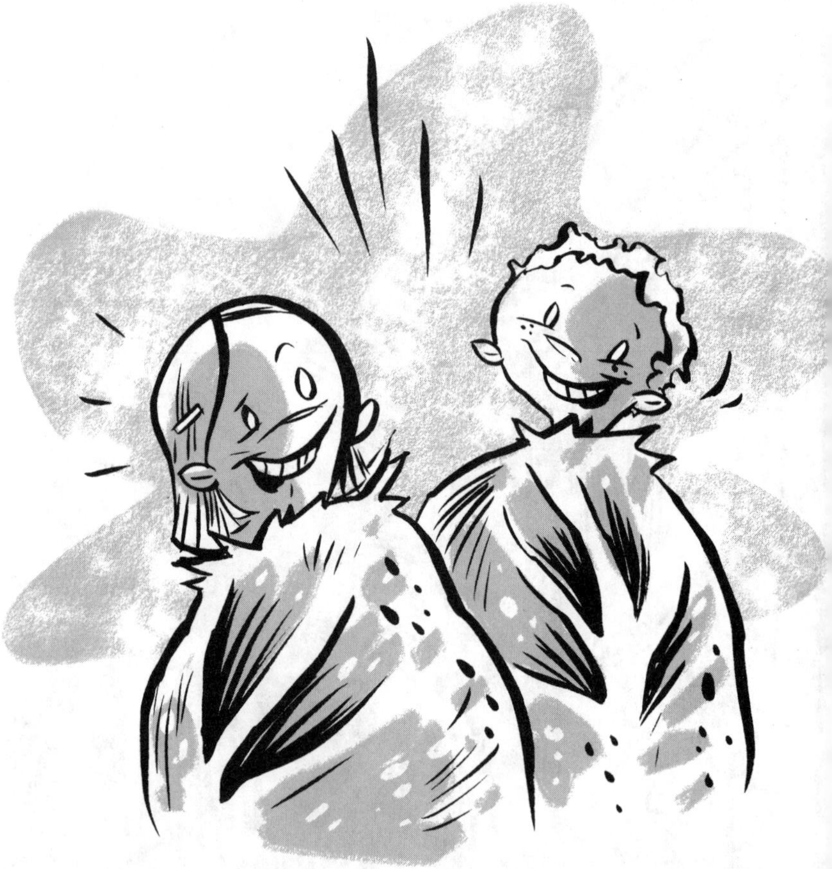

Produce uprising. No one but Jo Jo had seen him, or the villains, at all.

"What was all that racket?" Mikey asked with wide eyes.

"Yeah, it sounded like a tornado out there!" Ellen agreed.

"What did you two do, eat your way through so you could stick your heads out?!" Jo Jo laughed.

"Yeah." Mikey blushed. "We had to do *something*!"

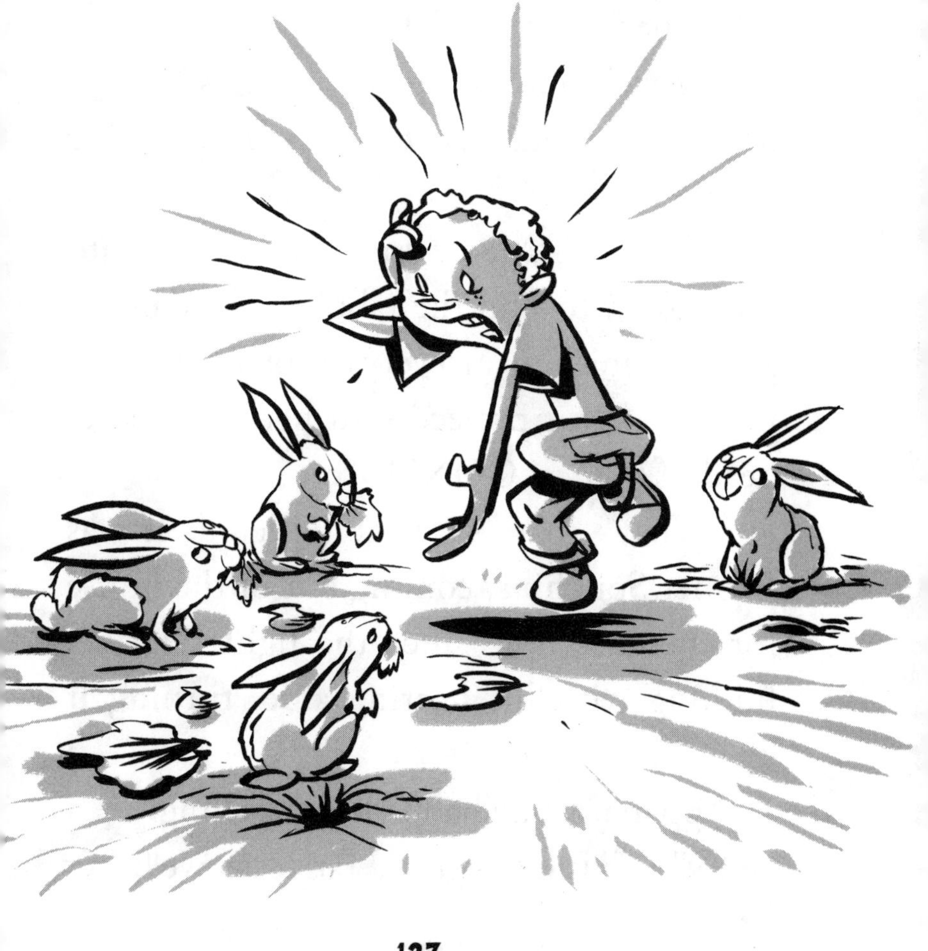

"We would've kept going," Ellen contin- ued, "but we needed salad dressing."

"Well," Jo Jo began to explain as she freed them from their leafy cocoons, "you two had the same idea as Farmer Spuchins' rabbits!"

"Whaddya mean?" Ellen asked.

"They broke out of their cages," Jo Jo fibbed, "and totally ATE our record-breaking lettuce!"

"WHAT?!" Mikey cried. He ran out into the garden to find the rabbits still hopping around, finishing up every last bit of greenery in sight. "Our project! Our perfect, perfect head of lettuce! GONE!"

"What's that?" a voice hollered. It was Farmer Spuchins, coming out of the house for the first time since the fight. He was fiddling with his hearing aide, turning it up.

Apparently, he hadn't heard a thing!

"Well," Ellen sighed, "at least we'll get

the grades we deserve for not doing the assignment properly."

"You never know." Jo Jo raised her eyebrows. "We might get extra credit for fattening up Farmer Spuchins' rabbits!"

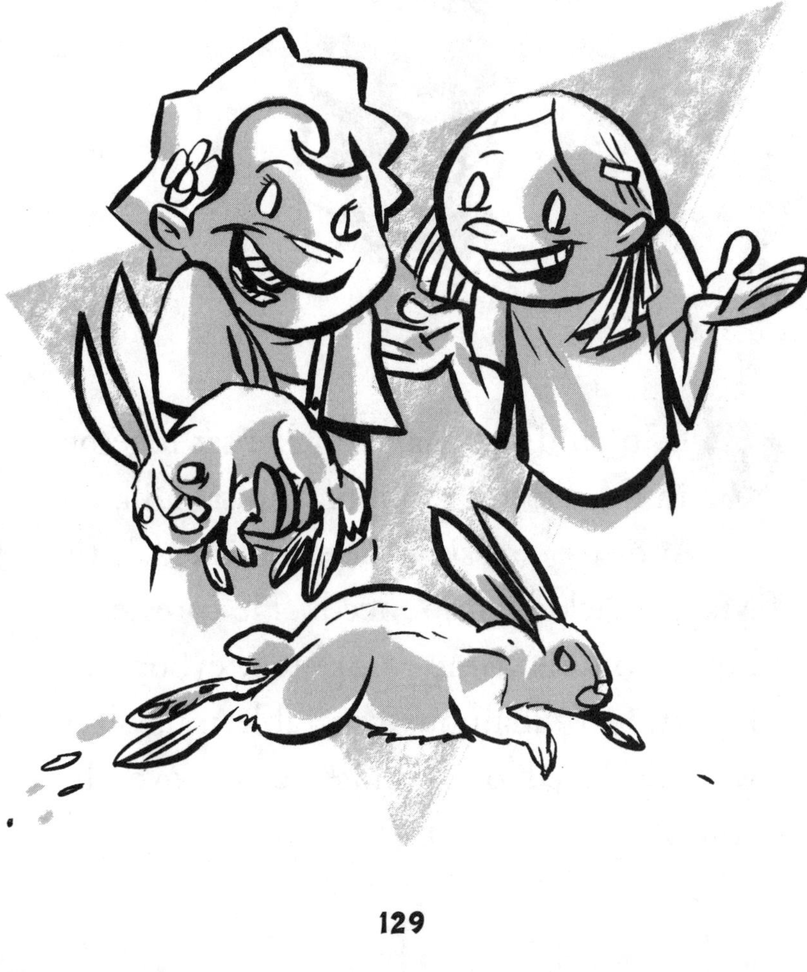

Chapter 11

Jo Jo and the Magic Pickle sat together in the control room of Capital Dill.

"Another mission accomplished," the Magic Pickle announced. He pressed a button on his crime computer keyboard. A big grid of villainous vegetable mug shots was displayed on a huge screen over his console.

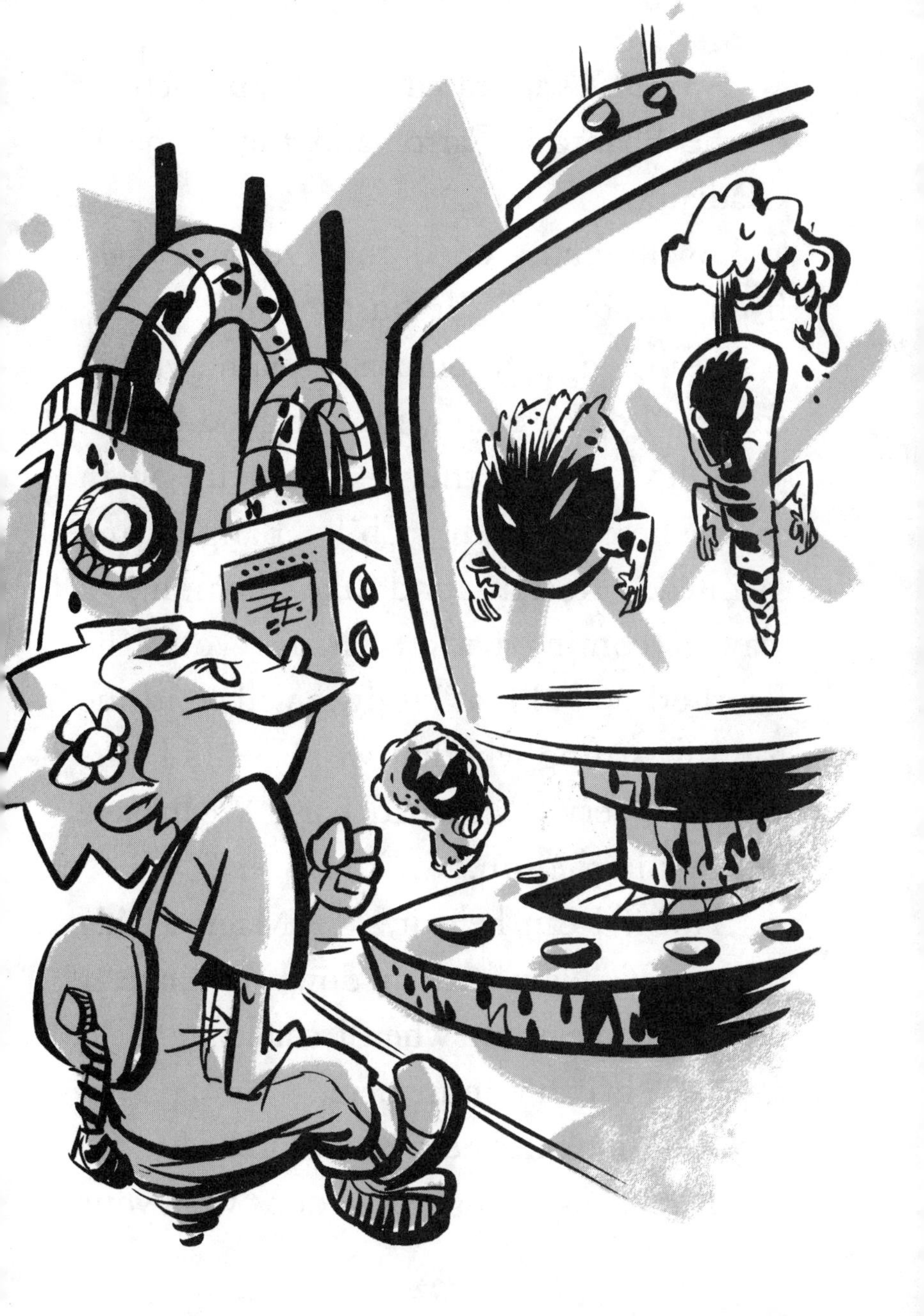

Two red X's appeared through the pictures of the Phantom Carrot and the Romaine Gladiator.

"Bwuhuhuh!" cried the Onion Ringer from a nearby cell. "It's just so sad!"

"Yeah," agreed Squish Squash with a frown. "I didn't even get to say good-bye."

"Oh, I'm sure they'll sprout up again somewhere." Chili Chili Bang Bang grinned. "Rotten food like them has a way of coming back to haunt you. The Brotherhood of Evil Produce will continue to grow strong whether we're behind bars or being served in salad bars. We'll have our day in the sun. . . . You'll see!"

"Not if I can help it," the Magic Pickle promised. "Now keep it down in there. I need to concentrate when I challenge Jo Jo to checkers in a minute here."

Jo Jo shook her head and grinned.

"No way," she laughed. "I don't want your

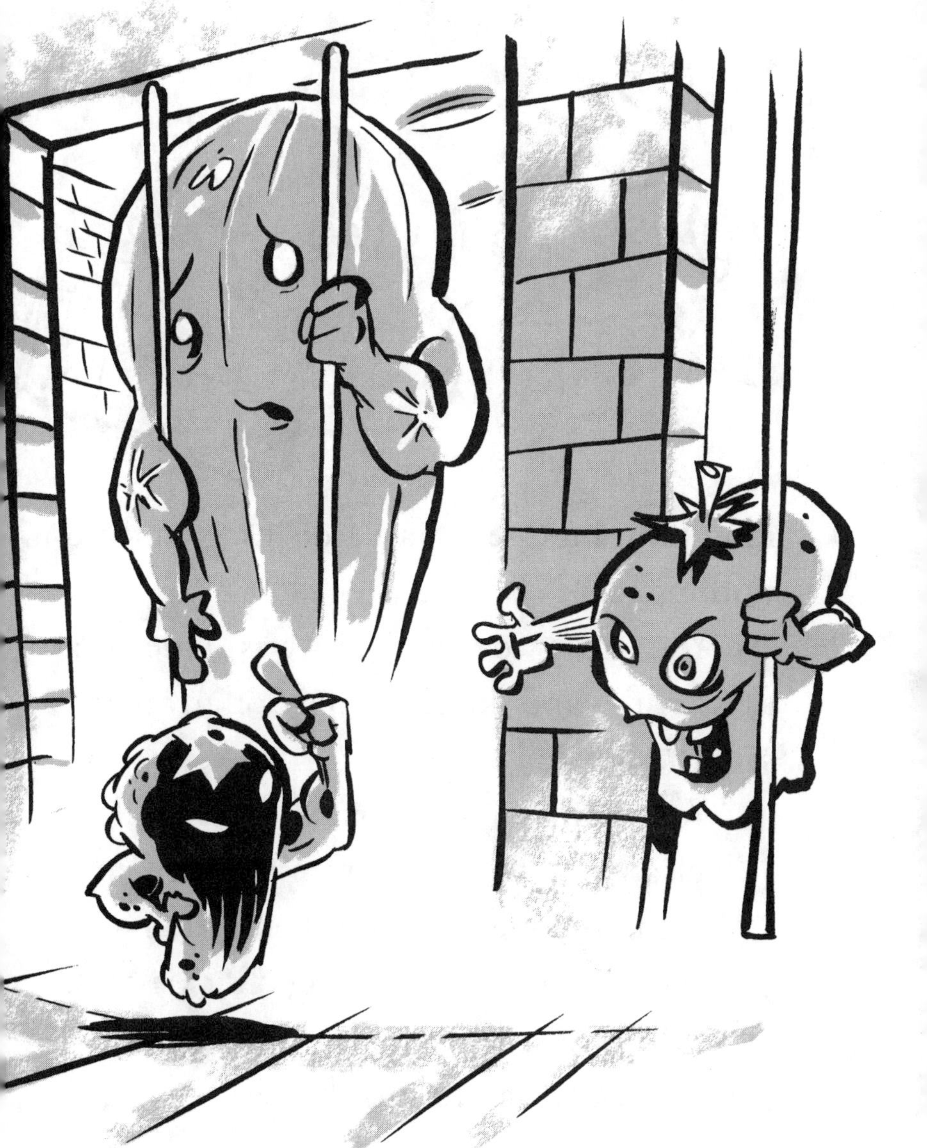

king jumping me so fast I disintegrate into nothingness!"

"You have to admit it was indeed a masterful—and skillful—move on my part," said the Magic Pickle.

"You've made your point," Jo Jo smiled. "I'll clean my own room from now on."

"Well, I hope your mother allows you your choice in pets," the Magic Pickle said. "I would suggest perhaps a rabbit. They've proven useful allies in the war on evil produce."

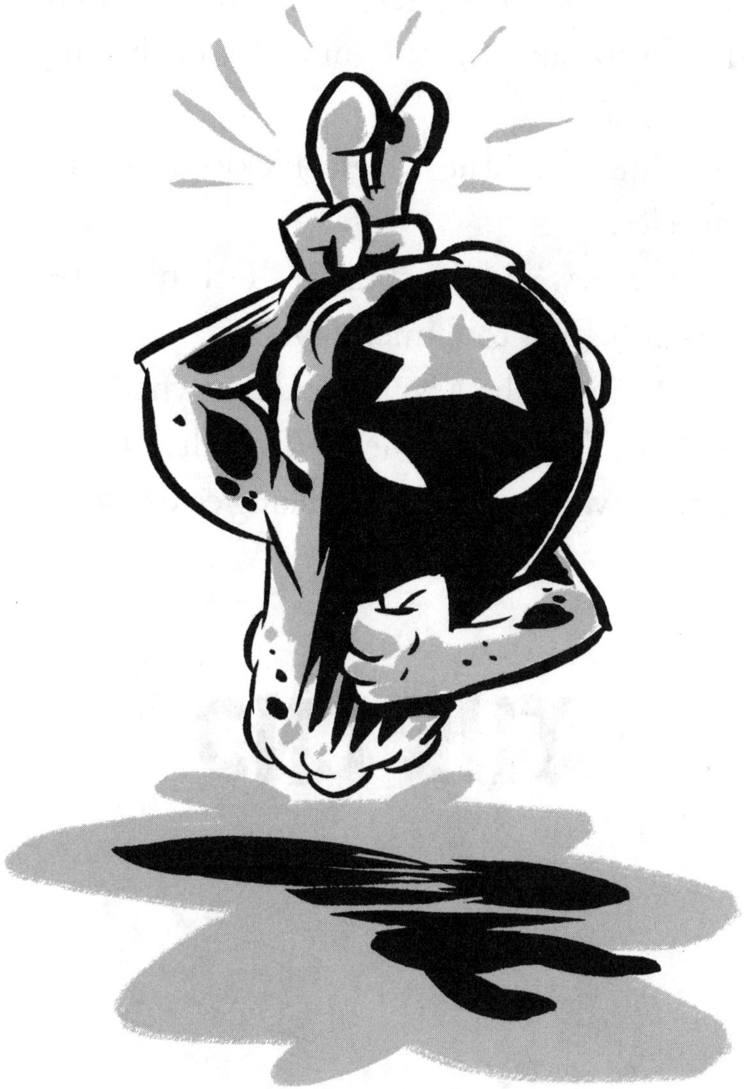

"Naw." Jo Jo shrugged. "I'd worry it might decide to take a nibble out of your bumpy ol' noggin."

"Unlikely." The Magic Pickle flexed his muscles.

"Besides." Jo Jo smiled. "I think a pet would be *way* too much work."

"Really?" The Magic Pickle frowned.

"Sure," Jo Jo replied. "I've already got enough work on my hands taking care of you!"

THE END

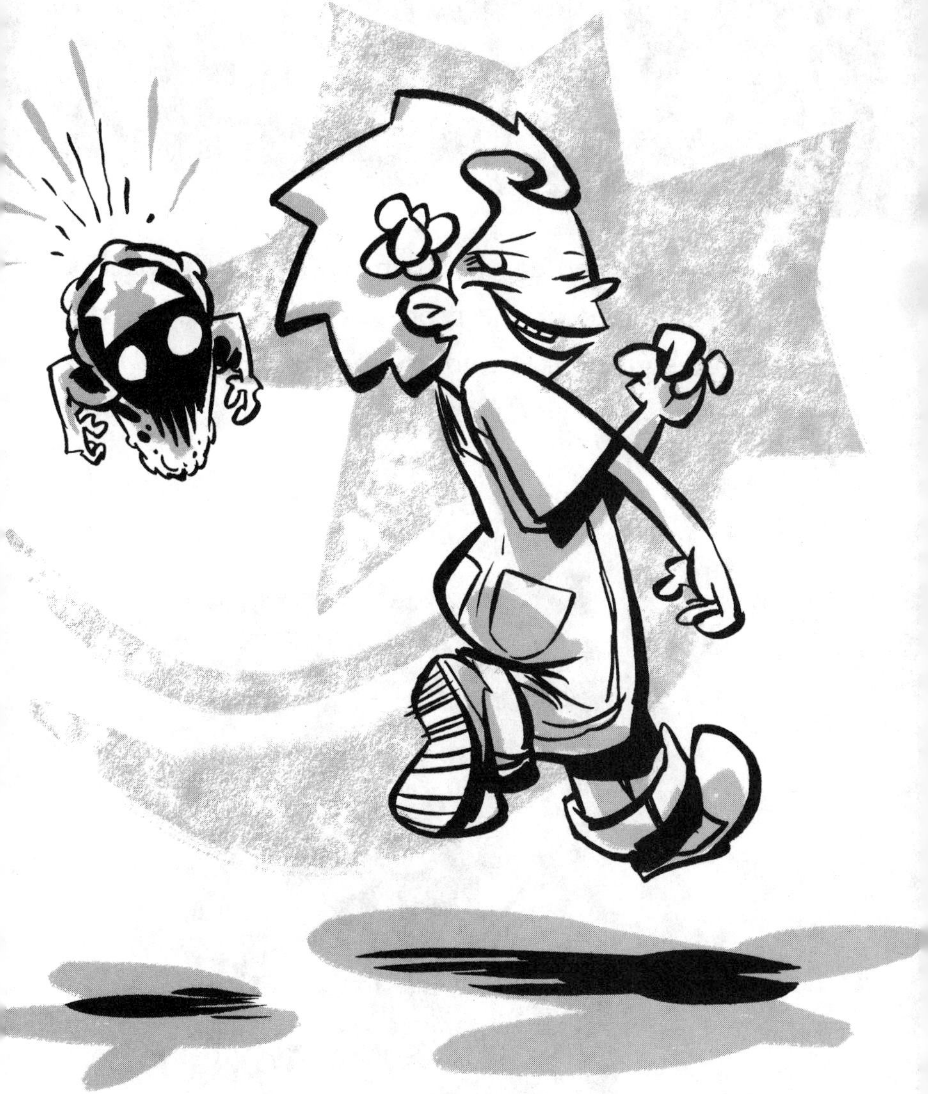

GO GREEN!

There's a rotten egg in town who's out to poach a wild kiwi but in the process creates havoc at the zoo. Magic Pickle and Jo Jo are on it in *Magic Pickel vs. the Egg Poacher*!

A graphix Chapter Book

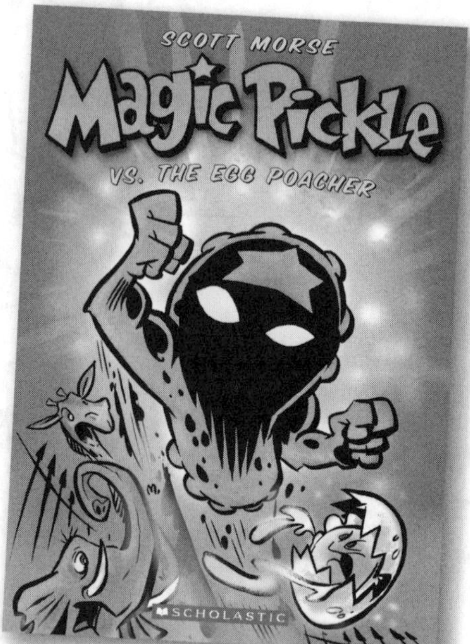
SCOTT MORSE
Magic Pickle
VS. THE EGG POACHER
SCHOLASTIC

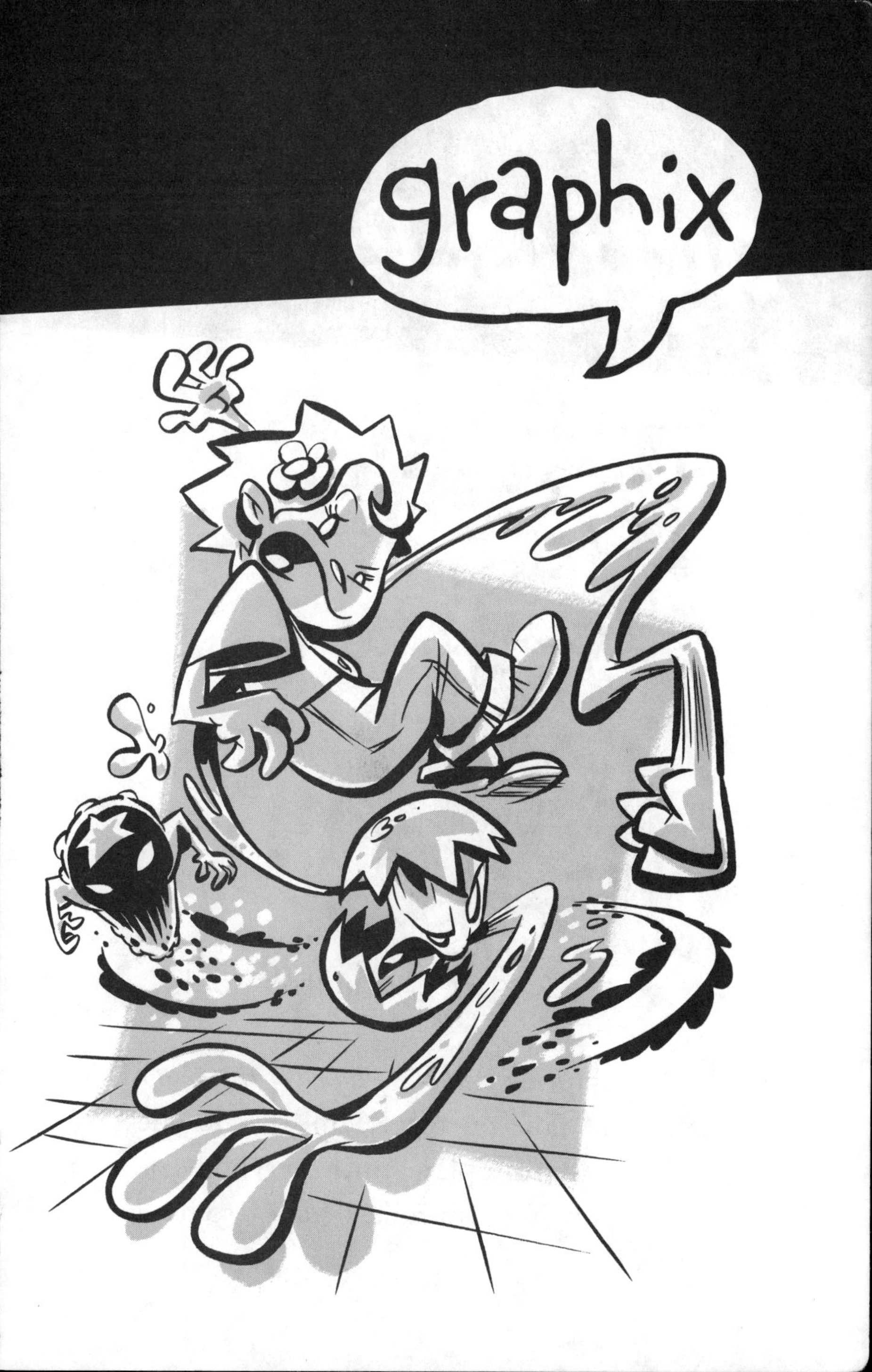
graphix

DILL VS. DANGER

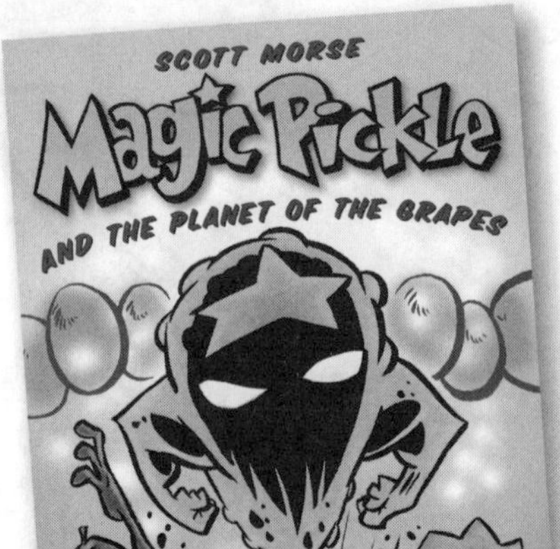
SCOTT MORSE
Magic Pickle
AND THE PLANET OF THE GRAPES
SCHOLASTIC

A graphix Chapter Book

In *Magic Pickle and the Planet of the Grapes,* MP and Jo Jo take on the Razin', a renegade raisin with a dastardly plan: turn everybody on earth into plump, juicy, mindless grapes, so he can rule the world.

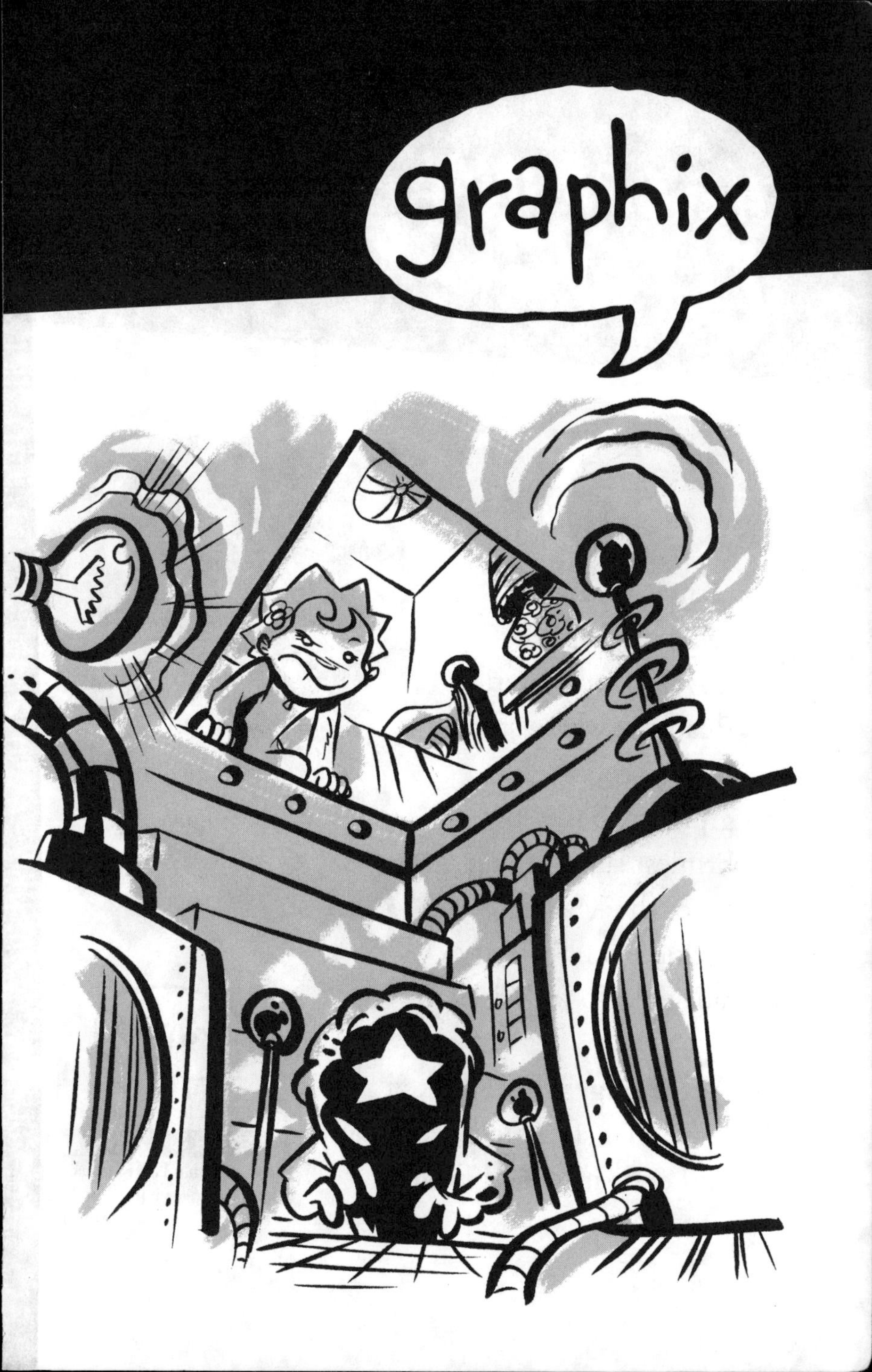
graphix

THE ORIGINAL FLYING DILL HERO!

Here it is: the original **graphic novel** in full color! Read the whole story behind the world's greenest, bumpiest, briniest super flying hero, the Magic Pickle, and his feisty sidekick, Jo Jo Wigman!

A thrilling, action-packed story that starts in a secret lab and ends in a food fight!

MORE PICKLE POWER
COMING SOON!

A (graphix) Chapter Book

There's something funky in Jo Jo's new school desk: an old peanut that won't stop glowing. Time to call in MP. Watch out for *Magic Pickle and the Creature from the Black Legume*!

Meet Scott Morse

If you read Scholastic's *Goosebumps Graphix: Creepy Creatures*, you saw Scott's super-cool art in *The Abominable Snowman of Pasadena* story (and if you haven't read it, check it out!).

Scott is the award-winning author of more than ten graphic novels for children and adults, including *Soulwind*; *The Barefoot Serpent*; and *Southpaw*. He's also worked in animation for Universal, Hanna Barbera, Cartoon Network, Disney, Nickelodeon, and Pixar. Scott lives with his loving family in Northern California.

And sometimes — if there are any in the fridge — he even eats pickles.